T0342798

THE OPPOSITE OF

DISAPPEARING

Short Stories in Uncertain Times

The Opposite of Disappearing

Edited by Laura Norris and R. A. Stephens 2021

ISBN: 978-1-76111-029-0

Published by Rhiza Edge, 2021
An imprint of Rhiza Press
PO Box 302
Chinchilla QLD 4413
Australia
www.rhizaedge.com.au

Cover design by Laura Norris and Carmen Dougherty
Layout by Rhiza Press

Individual stories are copyright to their individual authors.

The Suitcase by Deborah Huff-Horwood was previously published in
Better Read Than Dead's 2020 Anthology.

A catalogue record for this book is available from the National Library of Australia

THE OPPOSITE OF
DISAPPEARING

Short Stories in Uncertain Times

EDITED BY LAURA NORRIS
& R. A. STEPHENS

rhiza edge

Contents

Foreword

2020 was a year coloured by uncertainty. We put the call out for stories about how to adapt, how to thrive under immense pressure – to navigate a world turned suddenly on its head.

In response, the stories we received explored the idea that while uncertainty may present itself in different forms, the ways we answer are not dissimilar. It was telling that in a year where most of us were grounded both literally and metaphorically, a common theme of flight emerged – not just to escape the unknown, but to meet it.

After all, what is flight, if not a leap with no certainty of landing?

Laura Norris

When COVID-19 suddenly became what everyone was talking about, I found myself watching students, adults, family and friends confined to their houses. It inspired me to create an opportunity for something to do—to write! I wanted to use creativity to not only escape but extend people's imagination. In this collection the resulting stories consider how we go unnoticed, that we are just a part of something more and are all finding our way.

R. A. Stephens

Lines for Luca

D. J. Blackmore

Look at the birds of the air;
they neither sow nor reap nor gather into barns,
and yet your heavenly Father keeps feeding them.
Are you not worth much more than they?
Matthew 6:26

Israel was time rich. Destination unknown, he left the past at his back. A sunrise pooled between heaven and earth, then broke. A big breakfast sun, he tasted its warmth full in his face.

His head came up as something was thrown from a car. It whirred past him to roll away and stop dead. It was a pear. He stooped to pick it up. Brushing the specks off with his finger, he smeared a brown mark that tainted the flesh only just a little bit. But the fruit was ripe, the juice was sweet. It trickled down his chin like nectar.

It was an insult and a blessing at once, even though it had been thrown with a curse. Israel had learned to accept windfalls like this. The birds relied on fortune. He did the same. Earlier on, his wings had been clipped. He had begun to survive on providence. The gutter held more than the pockets of his coat, but he travelled light because of it.

Recalling the start of his journey, he guessed he had fledged from an empty nest. Now he walked with just the voice of his pen. No stutter ever came from a ballpoint, and that was a good thing. But the first time he had written words for someone, it had been for little Luca. His first poem, Israel had read to him because he had been too small to understand. On a docket from his pocket he had put down his rhyme. His brother had laughed and gurgled. He wished that he had kept it, but he could recite the words perfectly in his head.

***

People moved thick and sticky in the city streets. Israel's murmurs were no more than a coo amongst the doves as they went for the crumbs beneath commuters' feet.

No coal dust clinging to his clothing now, no grass seeds drifting from his hair. Here was the ether of soup kitchens, a thicker atmosphere. Israel smelled the chaos of cars, late opening bars, overflowing coffee grounds and salad scraps emanating from over-filled skip bins. They wafted their temptation of degustation outside side-street cafes. Eyes opening wider in the soft city light, Israel gorged himself with the sights.

He squinted at the sky but couldn't find the sun. It was somewhere in the vault above the skyscrapers, blocking the entry of the day's rays. Israel was beneath the firmament of the metropolis and he was spent. He lowered himself to a park bench and sighed. Between the slats of seating, a plastic-wrapped sandwich had been shoved, and Israel ate without guilt. Savoured every last crumb.

He took comfort in the company of strangers. He drank in their stories with a nod. Israel's eye traced the path of a rustling invoice. He bent and picked it up, then turning it over he started to write.

When the sky dimmed and noise was put to bed, crickets

2

chirruped, spiders crept. Israel put the poem in his port and stretched himself out, putting the pillow of the bag behind his skull. The weather was soft and the breeze was warm. He succumbed to the night and slept.

***

A shard of sun shone in his eyes. Israel turned his head to find his neck was kinked. Muscles cramped, and he realised that the bag that cushioned his head was gone. There was nothing but the endless isolation of grass.

He searched the streets for a police station. Stood irresolute before mounting the steps. Israel closed the glass door behind him tentatively. The bright glare of the police station held less warmth than a hospital. He wasn't well acquainted with either one. He took a moment to adjust to the temperature, fluorescent lighting, and his unease.

Coffee beans. He drank in the aroma as it hit his taste buds. His stomach imagined hot coffee, though he hadn't tasted a drop.

'What can I do for you?' A copper came from the next room.

Israel hesitated; his words faltered: 'I want to report a theft.'

The policeman's mouth was a handcuff of condescension, clamped shut. He took in Israel's appearance, recorded it as a mental note. Shuffled the papers on his desk, as if the place would be tidy when the stuttering dropout left.

The officer picked up a coffee cup that had once been white. Stains from satisfied slurps had run down the sides, like rivulets from one of those chocolate fountains Israel had seen in shop windows. His eyes were drawn to it, mouth watering in spite of himself.

'My bag's been stolen,' Israel said.

'What kind of bag was it?'

'It was a school case they took.'

There was a long moment before the policeman asked, 'Would you like to make a statement?'

'Yes, I would. I have to get it back.'

'Where did you lose it?' The officer put his head back and drained the cup, the elevator of his throat moving up and down, taking it to the lower level of his stomach. Israel swallowed. The policeman rubbed a hand over the taut shirt that tugged.

'In the park—one minute it was there, the next it was gone.'

'Is there any way you might have forgotten where you left it?'

'No.' Israel was emphatic. 'No, there's not.'

'All right, come into the interview room and I'll take down the details regarding your suitcase.' The officer opened wide the internal door to the room, leading the way.

'What kind was it?'

'The kind you take to preschool with your lunch in it.'

'Kind of little to hold your laptop, wouldn't you think? Valuables? Bank notes I expect.' It made the officer chuckle, but he didn't bother to look up from his pad. Teeth stained by bitter beans, dark as the mug on the desk, when the officer finally looked up to smile, it hit Israel like an insult.

'Far more valuable than that,' Israel said, turning to gaze through the window towards the street and away.

When he stepped out onto the footpath, the city hugged him with a rush of warmth, walking with him down the street. Its alleys were a lunch box crammed with familiar smells, reminiscent of orange peels, sandwich crusts.

A flurry of traffic raced through leaves where they swirled in the gutters. Dry day, it threw up the dust and flicked it into his eyes. Israel wiped it away. The place was full of people and prams—pigeons asking for alms. Their feathers every colour as they moved in glaring daylight. Israel was no different—a beggaring bird—only his clothing was not so brilliant.

A gust blew up the street, bringing lolly wrappers and shopping dockets. Israel put out a hand. Grabbed at a sheet of paper, watermarked from the gutter, wrinkled by the wind. He secured it in his pocket. Then down by the quay, he caught and folded another one.

A little girl held her mother's hand as they crossed his path. She turned her head to gaze at him.

'Don't stare,' her mother reprimanded.

'That boy's picking up the garbage.'

'Because so many people drop it,' her mother told her, hardly glancing his way, 'and that's why we use the rubbish bin.'

The girl gave him a backward glance. She smiled and waved before the corner took her curiosity and their steps. Then they were gone from his vision.

He had a pocket full of papers. Some folded, some way too small. A few were all coloured by advertisements, so much so that he found it hard to make out the marks of his pen at all.

***

The sun had moved its arm over the park. Israel was cradled by the bench in the lullaby of its warmth. When he finally awoke, the sun had left. He went to pick up his bag, but he needn't have bothered. It wasn't there. Anxiety grabbed at his insides like a hunger pang. He sat back as his stomach begged for ease.

'No, I didn't leave it in a toilet cubicle. Yes, there is a name written inside. Luca, that's what it says.'

How many times had he raked through the ashes of the past as though he could bring the days back? How long ago was it that he had reached down to take his little brother's hand? People's eyes had fed on Luca's disability back then, and Israel's anger had made a glutton of himself. But now, just saying the names of his family was almost enough to sate his sorrow.

There had been nothing to slake the flames.

Israel had become an orphan the same day he became a man. He had walked away after that. There had been nothing to stay for. Israel had begun a solitary journey, taking little but the silk of memories.

He had long since forgotten the shame of homelessness. Earning a crust meant different things to different people. Israel wrote stories. He penned the prose of people that passed, who never thought to look his way. A scraggly kid with a superhero lunch box filled with nothing but scraps.

He begged the beautiful out of the moments of passing pedestrians, pressing them onto the pages of forever with his words. He recorded a suitcase of emotions. Prisms of colour in the greyness of every day. He had guarded those words jealously; now even they had been consumed.

**

'Could I speak to the officer that was here yesterday?'

'I'm the relieving officer here today.'

'Have you heard anything concerning my suitcase? I—made a statement.'

'Were you given an incident number?' The copper was gruff.

'I know it's here somewhere.' Israel searched through his papers, through the words that filled his pockets. They spilled onto the floor. He fumbled to retrieve them with rising dismay.

'Listen, I'm too busy to have my time wasted.' Then in frustration: 'Do you want me to throw some of those bits of paper away?'

'No!' Israel was vehement. 'Here it is. I—found it.' He pushed it towards the officer. But there was nothing in the system that told them anything. Israel stood blinking, empty handed, blank as the computer screen. With a hollow heart, he walked away.

In the park, party balloons clustered one corner with colour. A backdrop of streamers and helium balloons. The fragrance of frankfurts and white wings of fluttering serviettes in the summer breeze. Israel sat like a bird. Magpies watched with curious eyes and snapping beaks.

A napkin dithered its way to his feet. Israel picked it up and set it down on his knee without thought. In front of him party hats were perched on curly heads. Elastic held tight around chubby cheeks, round with childhood and good eating. Faces shone with sugar. Mouths full of cake and laughter.

He drew their chatter with his pen. He caught their moments with his poem. A single flash captured in a memory of words. On the party plate of his serviette he piled the words high. An all-he-could-eat banquet, caught and held in two open hands, Israel savoured the lines.

'Would you like some birthday cake?'

He blinked. Israel searched the child's face and she smiled. Her mother pushed her a little closer. Prompted her daughter with an encouraging voice. The little girl held out a wedge of cake.

'I haven't eaten birthday cake in a while.' Israel put out his hands.

The girl's mother offered him a hotdog, almost apologetically. 'I don't suppose you'd like a hotdog, would you? We've got more than we can eat. I think I over catered,' she laughed. A magpie answered in kind, warbling above them.

Israel would have said *thank you*, but the words couldn't get past the bubble at the back of his throat. Emotion was like a big mouthful of fizzy drink that made his eyes water and nostrils sting. He had lost Luca's school bag. He had lost all he owned. Now here he was given a smile, some birthday cake and a sausage wrapped in bread. At that moment, he knew what it was to be rich.

When parents had packed up the streamers, the plastic cups and confetti, they herded the children together, putting babies into prams. Israel looked down at the napkin still clutched hungrily in his hands. He considered the words he had crafted before he approached the woman and the girl.

'I wrote this for you.' He knelt down and looked into the child's clear eyes. 'Happy birthday.'

The little girl accepted it with a smile and open hands. Like birthday cake.

'Thank you.' The woman met his glance and held it. It was something he didn't experience so much now days, and he smiled.

***

The noise of cars slowed the traffic's cadence. Bird chorus quietened as dusk approached. In the distance came laughter and the sound of something being kicked along the footbridge.

Israel squinted and stood, craning his neck to watch two youths approach. At their feet was a tiny suitcase. It was all he had left—Luca's port. From one to the other it went, between the hard caps of their boots.

It must have been the birthday cake that made him run like he did. The sugar that spiked his blood to pump fast. It beat thick and syrupy, a testosterone heat, because Israel was on the bridge, and he was trembling. His legs shook like jelly cups, but his shout was sharp and strident.

The boys stopped their school bag soccer. They stared as he came their way.

'Give me a look at that bag!' he ordered them. 'Let me see it, it is mine!'

They laughed, then the tallest kid picked it up and backing away, swung a leg and dropkicked it. The noise of their feet was already thundering away as the bag snapped open. It hit the iron railing and fell just shy of the edge. It burst into the air, and a white flock of paper doves rose in the updraft, before winging down to the river.

Israel stooped to pick up the lunchbox, dusting it free of dirt. He ran careful hands over the scratches, as though they were grazes on small knees. He opened up the little port and touched the words *This bag belongs to Luca.*

Then Israel stopped to cup his hands at the fountain where doves cooed. He drank deeply and sluiced his face. He sat down with the suitcase on his lap to watch the mourners at the cemetery nearby. From his pocket he selected a piece of paper. Not too big or yet too small, on the imperfect perfection of its crisp white surface he put down his words. He knew what grief felt like.

He was about to covet it as treasure in his bag. Instead he took it to the funeral director standing behind the mourners.

'Would you give this to his wife and—family, please?'

'Are you acquainted with them?'

'No, but I have some words I'd like to give.'

Then Israel crossed over the bridge, walking beneath the trees with Luca's suitcase. The sandwich box was empty, but his heart was full.

It felt like Israel had walked side by side with hardship for so long that they were classmates. In some ways they were friends. But poverty was not just an empty stomach. He had learned that being destitute could be far more than an empty wallet.

Israel travelled along the river. He walked the journey without knowing his destiny. He didn't know where he would be tomorrow, but he believed that good things were around the corner, whatever they were. Regardless of his circumstance, he'd been told once that joy was free.

Israel took the direction of the sun as a guide to his feet. The wings of his coat lifted with new freedom in the breeze. Some passing would only see a young vagrant, a homeless person on the street. Yet Israel had words to feed the hungry. His plate was full. He had stories to share.

The Opposite of Disappearing

Laura Norris

Hatch

The Eco Centre is a late addition to the university campus, a sharp left on entry. A sloped ramp connects a finger of land to the second-storey entrance and a verandah on the far side overlooks the bushland below. The entrance leads into a carpeted lobby and branches off into four conference rooms. The rooms are air-conditioned, but the main hall is not, and if the doors are left open too long, the hall, like a valve, filters in a blinkered, humid draft.

There are information touchscreens throughout the lobby displaying various information. Bird cams and life cycles. They are covered in the thumb prints of a quizzical young girl—Iris, six—who is darting between the cases.

Iris charts a figure eight course, which she replicates over and over again. Her hair is black and her eyes are long-lashed and spaced far apart. She is here to break the world record for running in circles without shoes. She is here to become a world famous explorer. She is here because her aunt, the entomologist, is watching her while her mum is in Singapore for work.

On her fiftieth lap, she crosses the imaginary finish line, arms stretched in victory. Her knees are shaky and she feels the beginnings of a stitch in her side, but she feels alive, superhuman. No one is faster than she is. She slows her breathing, hands on her hips. When no one is looking she pads over to the glass displays and breathes foggily on the glass. Uses her index finger to draw the perfect love heart and watches it rapidly evaporate in the heat. In the vivarium, a lone snake encircles lazily.

The centre of the room houses her favourite thing in the space: a dragonfly encased in amber. She loves the thin, delicate markings on its webbed wings, the tiny buds of its antennae. This is history. This is something precious stopped in time. And while it makes her sad to think of how the dragonfly made its sticky end, she thinks how cool is it that time can march on while it lies there, preserved in inexhaustible detail?

***

Unfurl

Iris bends her knee at the start line, feels her legs, solid, though a little shaky, beneath her. Her arms feel stiff, so she shakes them out. She is in lane two, placed next to two slow runners. No problem. It's lane four she needs to watch out for: Elodie Wright, tall, blonde, long-limbed and *fast*. Elodie went to Little Athletics after school and her dad was a soccer coach. Earlier that week, Iris overheard Elodie at the bubblers ranking her predictions for the 100m race. Elodie herself always listed at the top, the other Year Four girls, usually whoever was nearby, in varying, embarrassingly low placements. Iris bit her tongue. She had placed fourth in the practice run after a poor start and didn't want anyone to know she'd been practicing at home. Let them think she was an underdog. She could be *fast*, too.

In the split-second before the race begins, she feels a beating in her chest, something wild and winged trying to let loose. The tension lifts only when the starter gun *bangs* and she is hurtling forward with everything she has, the other runners a blur in her periphery. Eyes focused on the finish line and the row of cheering parents and teachers that line it. In the corner of her eye, she can see the mad swish of Elodie's blonde hair and she pumps her legs to match her speed, forcing air down her lungs. She hits the line half a second before anyone else does, her last push something magical, something close to flight.

The ribbon. The gold ribbon.

Elodie looks frazzled, undone. She tells anyone who can hear her, she was tired from practice yesterday; she wasn't trying really, and anyway, it's just a small race, who really cares?

Iris' breathing doesn't slow even after the ribbon is pinned neatly to her sports' shirt. The teachers line the girls up in a row: first, second and third, Iris in the middle. Right before the shutter clicks, Elodie turns to Iris.

'Honestly,' she says, 'I'm surprised you can run so fast with such fat thighs.'

The green field blurs. Iris doesn't react, though she later wishes she had something snappy prepared. *Sore loser,* she thinks to herself.

But that night, Iris looks at her legs in the bathroom. Sees them with new eyes. Wills them to thin.

***

Stagnant

The night before her first day of eighth grade, Iris stands in front of the mirror in her underwear examining her body. She has come to a realization. First, she is a poorly made first-draft. Like a sculptor clumsily shaped her body into something not quite finished. Second, there isn't a part of her she doesn't feel embarrassed for: the wide shoulders, the extra fold of fat at her lower stomach, her knobbly knees. Even her fingers are proportioned incorrectly, thick at the knuckles and squared at the tips.

She holds her hands (too big) to her face (too wide) and uses it to push her cheekbones up. She stares at her eyes which she eventually decides she is satisfied with. She remembers one of her friend's mums calling them almond-shaped. She liked the way it sounded then, how it made her feel special; the right kind of different. Now she hears it all the time, reads the same descriptions of girls like her in books: thin, almond-shaped, ivory-skinned. She wants to tell them there are other colours. There are shapes other than almonds.

Downstairs, she can hear the TV blaring, and voices rising steadily over it: her mum chatting to someone on the phone loudspeaker. From the room next to her, her brother is playing *Minecraft*. Nowadays, her dad works out-of-state and they each take their dinners to their respective rooms. Her aunt is gone too—working out of a nature reserve in the UK. It has been years since she's visited the Eco Centre and her memory of the building is distant, hazy at the edges.

A slight breeze pushes through the sliver between the curtains. Iris walks over quickly and fastens them shut. Her window on the second-storey looks down onto the street of a main road, which gives her the distinct feeling of being watched. In the distance, a strip of headlights cut through the dark.

Iris turns back to the mirror, holds herself up straight, and snaps a photo of herself on her new phone. She steps back from the mirror, adjusting her distance. Takes another photo, adds a filter, then flips it horizontally. The result is uncertain.

She analyses the photo, flips it again. Still no clear outcome.

She wants to be a backwards-written message. She wants to be held up to a mirror and deciphered into something new. The problem is, she stares so often at parts of her body that she can longer see it as a fully-formed thing but a collection of minor disappointments.

Iris deletes the pictures off her phone, then deletes them from her deleted folder. She does not want to see another image of herself.

She turns off the bedroom light and slides under the covers of her bed. When she closes her eyes, she can still see the afterimage of her body in the mirror. She lies completely still, listening to her shallow breaths, disgusted by the geography of her body. Outside her window, a car backfires, and her chest beats fast, then aches.

***

Motion

First period is cancelled and they are driving back from McDonalds in Jake's car, Iris in the backseat with Simone, the two boys in the front. They are not technically allowed to leave the school premises but, as Year Tens, Simone presses, they will be allowed to sign in late at the office and destroy the evidence (two Big Macs and two share packs of chicken nuggets.)

The windows are down and they are driving downhill loudly singing a pop song Iris half-knows the words to. The verses she doesn't know, she bops her head side-to-side instead, hoping her enthusiasm makes up for her inability to remember the words. She holds onto these moments. She has the feeling she is holding onto something fleeting, something precious.

Colt is sitting in the front seat directly ahead of her. As they crest the next hill, Iris puts her head out the window. Her hair is moving in what she hopes is an artful, wind-whipped way like a girl in a movie montage. When she puts her head back in, her hair is a mess. Simone laughs, musses it up even more. Colt hasn't looked up from his playlist, but he has to. She wills him to, needs him to see her at her best, her happiest.

This is how Iris wants to be seen: the right way, on her own terms.

They say goodbyes at C Block, and the boys and girls split. Simone hooks her arm through Iris' and grins, knowingly.

'So, Colt, huh?'

Iris feigns surprise. She'd thought she was being subtle.

'What do you mean?' she asks, but the words come out false.

Simone scrunches up her face and smiles. A look that signals being let off the hook.

Stagger

The change room is lit with overhanging, swinging bulbs—one rapidly blinking—so that the light in Iris' stall is, at times, suddenly shadowed. A fan is oscillating just outside and the curtain fabric, too short to reach either end of the stall completely, moves in and out like the room is taking a deep breath. In and out, in and out. The space is poorly designed. To enter meant squeezing past a rack of hanging, discarded clothes. Iris had the odd sensation when entering the change room of being digested whole.

'Have you got it on yet?' Simone's voice echoes from the stall next to her.

'Not quite.'

Iris unhooks the dress from the hanger. It's something Simone picked off the rack for their Year Eleven dance: a red, slinky wrap-around with a slit down the side. She pulls it on, feeling like she's pulling a giant sock over her body.

It fits terribly, she thinks. Or maybe it doesn't. There is something about seeing her body in a foreign space all lit up that horrifies her. All she can see are the ways her body doesn't fit together. (Too lumpy, too showy, too *much*.)

Iris feels the tears coming. She knows it's not as if she is completely hideous. She knows she is lucky to be the way she is now; she is told this all the time by her mother, her teachers, the internet. Someone in Africa is starving, someone in South East Asia is suffering. She cannot yet connect the discomfort of these platitudes with the knowledge that these people—always the unidentifiable 'they'—do not exist to make her feel better about herself. She knows she is lucky, but she also knows that she could be a little happier: *if only this could change.*

'I love this,' she hears Simone gasp. 'Okay, I'm coming out. You come out, too.'

'It doesn't fit,' Iris blurts out, immediately untying the knot at her waist, stripping the dress off in several awkward movements.

'Oh, seriously? Do you want me to find a different size?'

'No, it's okay. I don't think they had one in my size, anyway,' Iris lies.

There is a pause and she knows Simone doesn't quite believe her, but she also isn't one to press.

'All good. I'm just going to take some photos and then I'll change back.'

The lightbulb blinks again, sways.

***

Emergence

They are climbing Elephant Rock; Iris, Simone, Colt, Jake, Oliver and Audrey. The boys gallop upward, sure-footed, while the girls giggle and grab each other for support, scrabbling at sharp points in the rock for grip. Iris falls back. She is the only one not wearing her togs; they'd been in the water earlier and she'd volunteered instead to watch their things, feigning bad stomach cramps.

Instead, she'd flicked through a *National Geographic* her aunt sent her with an article on the slow extinction of dragonflies. Loss of wetlands, insecticides, pesticides. Reading and re-reading a line about dragonflies making the most of their sunny intervals, liking the turn of phrase; an image of them flittering in ephemeral sunshine. She took a photo of that page on her phone. In the distance, her friends disappeared into the surf.

Colt is darting up and down the rock, when he stops, smiling, and holds out his hand to help Audrey up. He helps the other girls up too, but there is something hollow, rehearsed about this follow-up gesture. Iris feels a sinking inside her.

At the top of the rock, despite the layers of clothing, her arms goose. In the sand, rows of red and yellow flags ripple upright. Somewhere in the distance, the faint whistling melody of an ice-cream truck. The group take a selfie squished together, salt-covered and wind-swept, throwing up peace signs. She sees Colt with her arm draped around Audrey's shoulder and her own image staring back at her from all the wrong angles. (Too squinty, too sandy.) Iris smiles, dying a little death, and understanding that this, too, is a kind of extinction.

***

Flight

Iris does not trip on her way up the stage to receive her high school diploma, although she envisioned it happening for the past forty minutes of speeches. There is a cheering from the crowd and she knows it's her friends: Simone, Colt, Jake, Oliver and even, begrudgingly, Audrey.

She takes the prerequisite photos with her parents and brother in the carpark. She exchanges words with her favourite teachers and makes shallow promises to keep in touch with her classmates online. At the edge of the crowd, Jake turns to their group and lifts an eyebrow.

'Let's hit the beach.'

They're in the car for forty-five minutes and Iris, in the backseat, singing loudly to The Killers, finally feels like she's getting her movie moment when she remembers the words to the entire song.

In the pizza place near the beach, they play darts in the corner—girls vs boys—and Iris, to everyone's surprise, hits the board every time with sharp throws that gravitate closer and closer towards the middle.

'How are you doing that?' Colt asks, surprised. His arm is around Audrey's shoulder again and Iris is pointedly trying not to notice.

She shrugs.

'I have never known you to be this coordinated,' Simone comments, and Iris laughs, because this is a skill she, too, didn't know she had.

As the sun sets lower in the sky, the boys chase each other into the surf, pulling off their shirts and tossing them onto the sand. The girls, giggling, strip out of their uniforms, down to their bra and underwear. Iris freezes.

'I'll watch your things,' she says, automatically.

'Seriously?' Simone looks disappointed. 'Just shove it in the car.'

Iris just shrugs, sheepishly, wishing she could explain without disappointing them. She takes her shoes off and watches them dive into the incoming tide, laughing riotously. The sand is still lukewarm beneath her toes. A gull cries overhead.

She is thinking about how her time in high school has been divided into moments like these, unequal parts of joy and exhaustion. All the versions of herself on the sidelines, waiting and watching. She watches them splash each other, thinking how it looks from afar as if they're fighting; some frantic, animal thrash that separates life from death. She wants more than anything to be where they are, in their unknowable future. To live out her own brief sunny interval. It was lucky enough to find people who liked her the strange, stilted way she was.

'Iris!' Jake calls out. 'Get in here!'

She wants to go in, but she'll need to take off her clothes.

'Iriiiis!' they yell.

She waits for them to turn away to unbutton her white shirt, unzip her culottes at the side. *Just for a few moments*, she promises. No one will see anything once she's in the water. The beach was already gathering dark.

Iris beelines to the water, clumsily mistimes her first steps and is hit face-first by a wave. She tastes salt, feels it up her nose, coughing, but picks herself up immediately. She plants her feet apart to push up. Some old muscle memory. The water is freezing, but how good it felt to cut a path like that, to run the way she used to before she became weighed down with the mechanics of her body. Underwater, she is slow-going but she feels confident enough to push through. (So quick, so *strong*.) How strange to think she's spent a lifetime at war with herself, treating her body like a specimen, prodding and dissecting, focused so long on what it should be, that she'd forgotten what it could *do*.

These are the muscles that hold her to the sand. Here are the thighs, the calves, the toes that propel her into the waves. Here are the hands, the joints that wade sharp lines through the whitewash. Here are the lungs that howl with joy.

'IRIIIS!' they call above the swell, out of her line of sight.

Head above water, she treads until they reappear.

If this were a moment in time lucky enough to be suspended in amber, it would show a figure appearing to the world as an immoveable force. It would show a girl squaring up against the sky and the sea, yelling: *I am here I am here I am here.*

The Suitcase

Deborah Huff-Horwood

Open it. You want to; it cries out for touching. See the worn fabric glued to cardboard, the leather corners cracked after all these years, the brass buckles? The handle has been repaired, a home job probably, for the stitching is a different colour. It had paper labels, but they've worn or been pulled off, though the glue still remains, long rectangles of powdery white. This suitcase went places, witnessed history, moved on. This suitcase once partnered a life.

***

Imagine a train platform. Steam rising, whistle blowing, folk scrambling to board, a few heart-rending farewells. Felt hats and luggage, wartime serge suits, fierce dogs on short leashes held by black-gloved men in uniform. '*Hurry*,' your heart calls to them, urging them aboard. 'Save yourselves.' Not quite aware that they would be saving you too, for they haven't yet met, your grandfather and his bride; you are not even a possibility. And while you know he does make it, there is panic in your eyes. You search for him in the crowd, there he is, thank God, hobbling along with his cane, dressed like the others, face inscrutable, suitcase in hand, boarding just as the conductor blows the final whistle. You shut your eyes and urge him safe.

The suitcase in your kitchen stands straight and firm. It has seen so much, but it hasn't bent, hasn't broken. *You are bent and broken*, says the voice in your head; *take strength from this case. You can endure. Step towards the suitcase, don't be afraid, lift it up and feel its weight. Open it, you know you want to.*

***

Imagine a room. Small space, narrow bed, thin cotton bedspread and a slim book near the pillow. A child-size wooden desk and chair. The suitcase waits at the foot of the bed. Thick blackout fabric has been pushed aside at the small window; outside it's a grey day. Where is this? Where is he? The door rattles as a key is turned and he comes. He looks exhausted. Gaunt; when did he last eat? He leans his cane against the doorframe. Eases his thin overcoat off his shoulders and looks for somewhere to hang it; with no hook or wardrobe he lays his coat neatly over the back of the little chair. Sits carefully—he's in pain, you can see it now—on the edge of the mattress. Closes his eyes to the agony of bending and removes his scuffed lace-up shoes; one of the laces has broken. Sits tall again, pale. Opens his eyes. Looks now at the suitcase, cannot tear away his eyes. Weariness layers his face like the tide; it looks like he has crossed the seven seas, crossed the world. He reaches an arm forward, rests a hand upon the flat of his suitcase. Brings his other hand over to manage the clasp. You feel in breach of his privacy and turn away. *I wish you'd watch.*

Secrets. You feel weak at the thought of opening yourself. *You haven't been able to share yours, that's your problem. So you live through others, absorbing their lives to dull your edges.* You know you should try, but you can't. *If it weren't for him, well, where would you be? You owe it to him to watch. I can promise you; it is okay. Don't be scared.*

***

You look at the case in your kitchen. You circle it, size it up. It is a small case, they'd call it cabin size these days, and though you don't know it, you will take this case and fly with it—fly—in years to come. Your grandfather boarded no planes, his flight to freedom was by land: trains and ships, automobiles and walking, lots of walking. A refugee, on the run with his careful plodding steps measuring the space between peril and peace. He'd cut the labels from his clothes so he couldn't be traced, couldn't be pinned to a country, couldn't be labelled 'enemy' by the enemy. Smart—brilliant, in fact. *Like you—if only you'd realise it. He knew what to do and he did it, alone, on his own. Think of that.*

***

Imagine him sitting by the train window, rattling through the long night. Cheap hat, for his other hat spoke of breeding, of place. He wears a wool coat, some warmth through this Europe winter. His socks thin, his shoes polished to a sheen with a handkerchief every morning, doesn't miss a beat. No mud on him, but no wealth either. His watch is a poor replacement, for a month ago he posted his father's. He carries a cane for his polio but with none of the markings of his class. Perhaps he reads a newspaper, perhaps he sleeps, bolt upright, ready to defend, to bluff and parry. *'You must get through, you must.'*

'Help! Is anyone a doctor?' And he'll close his eyes against the agony, time after time, but anonymity gives power, brings safety forward. He wants to write his future, not have it scripted for him. But not here, not now, no copperplate script from a gold-nibbed fountain pen writing prescriptions or long letters in Kings' English, no. One day he'll write that letter. *And one day you'll read it, my boy, one day you'll read it, the letter to his bride, his story.* Fleeing Europe, he sits with a straight back and wills himself forwards, writing his story in his mind, through the dark hours of history.

***

You reach down and wrap your fingers around the handle of the case. It is comfortable and subtly warm like holding someone's hand;

a comfort to hold. *Your grandfather gripped this, ran with it, tossed it and himself on the mercy of strangers, wagered himself and this—which was all he had, imagine that—on his instincts and contacts. Friends in far places, friends never met. Trust. It is trust that is key.*

***

Imagine him in the night, on another train, the lines of his forehead etched deep and quivering ever so slightly as yet another city approaches. He must be right to panic; he must know something. *'Do something!'* you murmur. The train slows, just a little; if he hadn't been wide awake he'd have missed this silent easing of the brakes. There are only a few lights across the valley, farmhouses most likely, and he must know the station will be patrolled with ugly-hearted guards who will board and check each passenger before the train can move on again. People are always taken away, guns at their back.

Once, he watched a woman he had talked to briefly, leap from the train as the guards approached, and she'd seemed such a reasonable person. Strangers with stories; he has learnt not to share. *But you have a story, or are you forgetting? You should tell it; it's not wartime now; trust someone.* He has risked it before, those guards. But not tonight, he feels a disquiet. Stands amongst the sleeping, silently moves to the door that opens to the small landing between the carriages, slides it open as quietly as he can, eases himself and his suitcase awkwardly through the gap. Beside the track is pasture, he knows that much, and hopes it is soft, cannot see. The lights of the town are still a few miles away. Wiry without food, your grandfather clutches his case and jumps.

Will he be missed from the train? He'd made sure to keep moving from his seat, tapping his breast pocket so fellow passengers would think he was off for a pipe. Went to tip his hat to a well-dressed woman and had to check himself, there's no hat now, the breeze blew it off and who knows, she could have been a spy. He lives by instinct. Leaping from the train into a field is a sensible thing to do, his gut tells him, and he's a doctor, he listens to bodies so trusts what his says. Never mind he's an ear, nose and throat surgeon; he draws knowledge from within and right now he's clutching his bag and stumble-rushing, gaunt as he is and with his polio, across this field towards the closest small light where he hopes he'll find eggs and maybe some vegetables. Bread cooling on a window ledge, if his god is truly smiling.

***

Your palm cradling the handle, you lift the case. Its lightness surprises you. You had thought it would be heavy with learning and sorrow, leaving his university post in Vienna as the trucks rumbled and the news grew black. Books were being burnt, people being turned from their jobs and their homes, shops once trading were shut overnight. The stars fell and were trapped on armbands and wept. *But think: what could he carry to a new life that wouldn't give him away if he was searched? Not tools or books or letters …*

***

Imagine looking at the photo. Carrying this is the greatest risk, and but he believes he can talk his way out of it. A gracious woman with her hair all done up and pearls at her throat and him, the tiny boy, seated stiffly by her side. When he is searched and grilled by guards on another train in weeks to come he will tell them she ran the orphanage. 'It's the only picture I have of me as a baby.' The guard will think him pathetic and crumple it in his fat fist and throw it to the floor, but he'll reach for it and live. His mother raised her family, son after son, saw them conjugate their verbs and learn their algebra and excel at everything, for she knew knowledge is power. Someday he will frame this photo in heavy silver to place on his mantlepiece beside photographs of his new bride, who will stand beside him smiling at her beloved new husband as a little man, imagining their babies will look like him, but with less lace. *And more smiles*, you think; *more smiles*.

Did she love him, you wonder? You stare into her gaze, but she shows nothing, and your little grandfather looks wooden and tired-eyed in this photo; there's no joy in either of them. But you know the photo was in the suitcase, you can feel it in your bones. With careful hands you place the suitcase on your bed, for you've walked from the kitchen to your room, you need the comfort. Softness, carpet, a gentle place to lay down this treasure. What he went through you'll never know, it's all imaginings, stories in small grabs from family, and you're young, you've not thought to ask. But you have this suitcase. The lawyer called last week to arrange delivery of your inheritance. Why you, is anyone's guess.

***

Imagine the suitcase in his home, filled later with tumbling children, two boys and two girls, your father among them. Was it stored in a cupboard? Under the stairs? Filled with old schoolbooks or knitting? Was it scuffed and forgotten, or jumped on with glee, or a playhouse for kittens? Perhaps it held papers, accounts for his house, or he kept it in his rooms on Macquarie Street among Sydney's other medical specialists. Imagine no more, for here it is, softly weighted on your blanketed bed.

You lay both hands upon the suitcase, fingers spread flat. Were this a piano, you'd be about to begin a sonata. 'Thank you,' you breathe, into the soft morning light. For he lived, and here you are. He kept his secrets and he lived, and from his marriage your father went on to have you. *But you? You have that secret. You need to let it go.*

You feel strangely ready now. There's a sudden urge to go places, it is time to move on. You place a call—*There, I knew you could*—then stand at the window and listen as a distant train passes by. You turn to the suitcase and undo the clasps.

Paper Crowns

Sam-Ellen Bound

My brother, Jesse, wants to be a Snow King, so I'm helping him make a paper crown. I've spent the last hour folding paper and cutting out snowflake patterns for him to colour. Once again it's me who has to watch him so Mum and Dad can 'enjoy the last night of ski season'. Rachel always gets out of it, probably because she's older.

It's hot in the lodge. Everyone's sweating out the spanakopita Grace Ambrosia made for dinner and Jesse wrinkles his nose.

'Yuck,' he says, 'It stinks.'

'That's all the garlic,' I say. 'No vampires welcome here.' There's a fine sheen of sweat around his forehead and his baby hairs are damp. I go to smooth them back but he knocks my arm out of the way.

'Cleo! You made me go out of the lines!'

I look at the crown, thick with crayon scribbles. 'Jesse,' I say. 'Snowflakes aren't red.'

Jesse considers the crown, his little tongue poking out. 'My ones are.'

'Why don't you do a bit of blue here?' I suggest, pointing, but he smacks my hand.

'Don't touch,' he says. 'You'll break it.'

'Course I won't. But even if I did, we can use some sticky-tape. Look, this cool one, with the patterns on it.'

But Jesse won't be swayed. 'Don't want sticky-tape, Cleo. Snow Kings don't have broken crowns. Then they can't be the boss anymore.'

'You're right,' I say, but I'm not really listening; I'm side-eyeing Jake Livingston and trying to think of a reason to go over to the wood heater where he's sitting with his friends. They're all drinking beer and every now and then one bursts out laughing and shoves the other. It's so cosy it makes my heart ache. Jake's older than me, he's probably even older than Rachel, but I think he's the funniest, and definitely, the cutest guy I've ever seen at the lodge. He taught me how to ski when I was eight and I've loved him ever since.

This year I figured something out. You have to be a *type* of person for anyone to notice you. You can't just be regular old you. You've got to be like my sister Rachel, who's pretty even though her personality is a dud. But she has long, shiny straight hair and dresses all boho and is into the arts, even though she can only play, like, three chords on her guitar. So it's like everyone *oohs* and *ahhs* over her pretty wrapping, but if they tore off the paper and nice ribbons they'd probably demand a refund.

I don't really know what type of girl I am, and when I try to be like Rachel I feel like that bad extra in a movie—you know, that awkward one who always over-acts, thinking someone will miraculously notice and make them a star. I've tried to be a bit funny and I've tried to be a bit mysterious and overall just cool and chill, so I can have my own thing that guys notice. You know, like I'm just one of them. Maybe it's worked because I swear these past couple of weeks I've seen Jake looking; not just like, looking, you know, but *looking*. Like he's interested. Like I've caught his eye.

Right now he's checking out something on his friend's phone

and his jumper's ridden up. I can see a little bit of his side, all smooth and caramel and muscly. I guess I make a little noise because Jesse looks up at me, crayon poised.

'Cleo,' he says. 'Guess what? You make your own crown. You can use blue.' He pushes another paper crown at me, the first one I cut which he rejected because 'the triangles weren't pointy enough.'

I colour in the whole crown in the time it takes Jesse to colour in one snowflake. I watch the way his eyelashes brush against the smooth pink of his cheek, the tiny little squares of his nails and the stocky way he holds the crayon.

'Stop watching me,' Jesse says, without looking up.

'Sorry, my King. I will ask for your permission next time.'

'Permission denied,' Jesse says, with a little squeal of laughter. Here's another thing I've learnt: you're irresistible when you have baby teeth.

I look back over at Jake and he's gotten up now, he's coming over to get a beer or something. I try to look world-weary and bored and casual, but also like a cute, attentive big sister. My armpits get all prickly and I press my arms against my side in case I have sweat patches. Jake catches my eye as he passes.

'Paper crowns, eh?'

'It's all happening over here. Party on.'

Party on, an icy voice sneers, in the panicky part of my mind.

The voice is right. I couldn't have said anything uncooler. I'm not sure what to do with my hands then, so I pick up my own blue crown and pretend to model it.

Jake laughs. 'Got one for me?'

'No,' Jesse says, and turns his shoulder away.

'Ten bucks and I'll do you a custom order,' I say to Jake's back, and he gives me a thumbs up and keeps walking to the fridge. I quickly take off the crown because I spent one and a half hours straightening my hair this afternoon so it looks like Rachel's, and I don't want to mess it up.

Jesse stares at me and scrunches up his face like a little troll.

'Your crown should cost one hundred dollars,' he says, and goes back to his last snowflake. 'Not ten. You're the Snow Queen, remember?'

Jake's carrying another six pack of beer on his way back and he acknowledges me with a little eyebrow raise. It's definitely a moment of connection.

Jesse finishes his crown and holds it up, triumphant.

'Look!'

'I can see,' I say. 'Very nice.'

'Help me put it on,' Jesse says. I tuck it over his head. It's a little too big and his ears are the only thing stopping it from falling around his neck.

'Should we tighten it up with some tape?' I reach around for the back, but he wriggles away.

'No! I like it.' He picks up my crown and holds it out. 'Now put yours on.'

'Nah,' I say, smoothing my beautiful, straight hair.

'You have to,' Jesse insists, and he grabs the ends of my hair to pull my head down.

'Jesse! Don't touch my hair!' It comes out a little angry and I see the shock start to creep over his face. I quickly put the blue snowflake crown on my head and jut out my chin, adopting a snooty expression. 'No one touches the Snow Queen's hair,' I say, as if every word has their nose pointing sky-high. Jesse laughs and tries to copy my expression.

'Or the King's!' He grabs a texta from the pile and points it at me like a wand. 'Or I'll turn you into a frog!'

'Jesse, that's a wizard, not a king. Kings don't have wands.'

'I do,' he says, and then he jumps off his chair and has a wand-fight with, like, an imaginary wizard or something. It's embarrassing and he's being really loud and I see Rachel look over and glare at us. The Snow Queen inside me shivers with annoyance. It's not like Rachel's doing anything but sitting there with her stupid friends and they're all on their phones, anyway. If she doesn't want Jesse to act like the five-year old he is, then she could always come over and help out for once. I mean, it's not like I don't have a life, too, outside of babysitting my little brother.

What life, the Snow Queen says, bored, and she's got me there. Babysitting Jesse *is* my life, and I'm not even that good at it. Only last month he had to go to hospital because I got him to make muffins with me and when he went to get them out of the oven I forgot to tell him to use a towel.

'Jesse, here! Have some M&Ms.' I grab the bowl of chocolate that someone's left on the breakfast bar. That shuts him up and he races over and scoops a big handful, wiggling his fingers about so he can get more. 'Jesse! Germs! Other people want to eat them too!'

But he's already off, one hand full of chocolate and the other holding his texta wand. He walks by Mum and Dad, who are carrying on with their friends, and points his wand at them. 'Bzz! Bzz! Frogs!' he declares through a mouthful of chocolate, pushing at the red crown that's fallen over his eyes.

'Jesse!' I chase after him.

'Bzz!' He buzzes me into froggy oblivion and wanders over to— of course he does—Jake and his friends.

'I'm going to turn you all into frogs!' he tells them.

'Is that right?' says Jake.

'Cool crown bro,' says another.

I rush over and grab Jesse's arm.

'Bzz bzz bzz!' he says, smacking me with the texta. There's brown and green smears on the sides of his mouth.

'Sorry about that,' I tell them.

'No dramas,' says Jake, chugging his beer and peering at me

over the end of the bottle.

'You're lucky you escaped with 'frog',' I say. 'People he doesn't like get turned into sea slugs. It's very unfortunate.'

'But I *don't* like them,' Jesse says.

Jake laughs at that and I feel my whole body radiate from one curly little point in my stomach. He nods at my head and I realise I'm still wearing the stupid blue crown.

'Where's my one?'

'Nah, blue isn't really your colour, bro,' says his friend.

'You can have mine,' I say, trying to remove the crown off my head and smooth out my hair at the same time. 'The original design. Definitely won't find that at Kmart.'

'Nice,' says Jake, and I hand my crown over to him, but it's me who feels like I'm the one being bestowed with a gift. He places the crown crookedly on his head and the Snow Queen watches him coolly, appraising. I can feel a single drop of sweat pooling at the waistband of my pants.

Jake looks round at his friends. 'Well?'

'Very handsome,' I say, and the other guys titter. One of them nudges Jake in the side.

'Thanks,' Jake grins at me, and then Jesse of course ruins the moment by tugging on my arm.

'Why'd you give him your crown, Cleo? Now you're not a queen.'

'I don't need a crown to be a queen,' I say, looking directly at Jake. Then I feel a bit sick because maybe that was a bit much, like too flirty or too much like a lame line from a movie. I don't know how to follow it up.

Anything? I ask the Snow Queen, but she's silent and serene, still observing with her ice-sliver eyes.

It's Jesse who comes to my rescue.

'I want more chocolate.'

31

'What the King wants, he gets,' I manage to stutter out, still looking at Jake, before my little brother hauls me away. Crap. What if Jake thought I meant him?

I stew on that for about five seconds before shrugging it off. No. I'm going to be confident. I'm the Snow Queen. There's no Rachel this time to steal my throne. It's my time to shine, to take charge. To be powerful.

Jesse gets more chocolate and romps around with his texta wand. We hide under a kitchen stool for two minutes while the 'bad guys' try to attack our castle. When we emerge, unscathed, Jake and his friends are shrugging on coats and scarves and beanies and going outside.

I'm not one hundred percent on it, but I'm pretty sure Jake gives me a smile just before he goes out.

Someone has built a big bonfire out there and you can see through the windows the glow of it roaring up into the sky. I wait a few minutes and then I check to see what Mum and Dad are doing. Still oblivious. Grace Ambrosia is making more spanakopita. Rachel and her friends are still on their phones. I hustle over to the lodge entrance, where no one in the main room can see you if you stand at the right angle.

I survey everyone's cold weather gear hanging up on the hooks. 'Jesse, where's your coat and gloves?'

'Why?' Jesse breathes on the glass panel in the door and then squiggles through it with his texta wand.

'Because we have to go outside.'

'Why?'

'Because look at that big fire out there,' I say, snatching his coat and beanie and then some gloves which I'm pretty sure aren't his. 'I think there might be a fire-dragon living in it.' Jesse peers outside and I know I've hit the jackpot. 'You could get it with your wand.'

Jesse turns around and bumps his bum against the door. 'Mum

said don't go outside tonight. It's too cold. I heard her.'

'She won't mind, plus it's only for a little bit. Just so we can see the dragon. Come on.' I hold out the coat. 'Jump in.'

Jesse makes a face. 'I don't want to,' he whines. 'I hate that coat. It's too hot.'

'I know it's hot in here, but out there—' I clutch my arms around myself and pretend to shake. 'Brrrrr!'

Jesse laughs and copies me. 'Brrrr!'

'That's right,' I say, holding out the coat. 'Jump in!'

'It's too scratchy,' he pouts. 'Like a rat skin.'

'Oh!' I feign surprise. 'I thought it was dragon armour.'

That does the trick, although he still wiggles and pulls at the collar and unzips it as soon as I zip it up.

'Come on Jesse,' I say, helping him with the gloves. There's still little puckers of red-white skin where he burnt his fingers on the muffin tray. 'Kings don't complain.'

That silences him but he bucks away when I try to put his beanie on.

'Don't crush my crown,' he says, so I have to take the red crown off very carefully, ram his beanie over his head, and then position the paper crown back on top.

'Perfect,' I say, turning for my own things. 'Warm *and* kingly.'

'So itchy,' Jesse complains, and he taps the coat with the texta wand. 'Bzz. Bzz.'

I don't put my own beanie on because I don't want to cover up my hair. I regret it almost immediately because as soon as we're outside the snow and wind are so cold it's like someone has stabbed the inside of my ear. My nose starts to run.

Jake's standing round the bonfire with his friends. Some of them are sitting on plastic chairs and there's girls sprawled all over their laps. One of the girls is Rachel's best friend. Two other people are standing on the far side of the bonfire making out.

'Yuck,' Jesse says, and points his texta at them. 'Bzz.'

'Shoosh,' I whisper, and he grizzles and tugs at his coat.

'There's no dragon here, Cleo,' he says. 'Let's go back inside. This coat's *itchy*.'

'In a minute,' I say, and then I catch Jake's eye.

'Now,' says Jesse. 'It's the King's order.'

I smile at Jake. He's not wearing my paper crown anymore; I think I can see a scrap of it in the fire. I'm sure the wind just blew it off and it was probably too late to save it.

Jake moves away from his friends and sidles closer to me. My heart is thumping like a drum, no joke, and it's like there's helium in my throat. I swallow it down and try to keep myself tethered.

'Hey.' Jake is all smiles, hands in his pockets.

'Hi,' I say, hoping the snow hasn't frizzed up my hair. At least with a coat on I don't have to worry about sweat patches. Jake gives me a little nudge with his shoulder.

'Hey Cleo,' he says, leaning close. I think maybe I can smell some of the garlic spanakopita but it's probably just leaking out from inside. 'Do you wanna go for a little walk with me? I want to ask you something.'

Oh my god. It's like my body has absorbed all the bonfire heat but it can't escape and I can feel the sweat gathering at my collar, behind my knees, on my back.

'Sure,' I say.

'Great.' Jake nods around the side of the lodge. 'Meet you back there?'

'Yeah in a bit,' I say, because Queens don't run on anyone else's time but their own, and Jake grins and shambles off around the side of the lodge. The dark swallows him very quickly. I look down at Jesse and dust the snow from his sleeve. 'I've gotta go for a minute, Jess. You be alright?'

Jesse lowers his texta wand. He watches the teenagers on the other side of the fire lapping up each other's spit. 'Why?'

'Jake wants to tell me a secret,' I say. 'And it's super-secret so we have to go where nobody else can hear, but then I'll be back and we can go inside and hunt some more dragons, okay?'

Jesse pulls at his coat, looks at the fire.

'But I want to know the secret,' he says. 'You have to tell me. I'm the King.'

I bend down so I'm at his level and adjust his red crown. 'Alright,' I whisper. 'I'll tell you if you're good and stay here.' Then a massive grin takes ownership over the whole bottom half of my face. 'It's gonna be a good one. A really good secret.'

He scratches at the hair poking out from under his beanie. 'Okay. The King says yes.'

'Thank you, your majesty,' I say. 'Don't leave this fire, okay, but also, don't stand too close. Stay right here until I come back. I won't be long.'

'Bzz,' says Jesse, lashing at a spark that's popped out of the fire. He points to where the trees begin, behind everyone's cars. 'Do you think some dragons would be over there?'

'No,' I say. 'And don't go looking. Wait until I come back. Promise?'

'Bzz!' Jesse says to another rogue spark.

I pat his head and follow Jake into the gloom around the side of the lodge. I go slowly, like a Queen would, unhurried, because this is a Really Big Moment. It could be the moment my life changes and I want to stretch it out. I want to hear the snow crunch under my feet and be infused with the soft light falling from the lodge windows; I want to feel how my nose runs, how my fingers tingle, how I'm finally going to have something just for me.

At the edge of the lodge I pause to check back on Jesse. He's watching me, his texta wand forgotten, his bright red crown all rosy from the fire. I give him a wave and then walk down the ramp to the back entrance, where everyone comes in from skiing. There's a snowmobile there under a tarp and Jake's leaning against it, in a weak orange cough of light. The piercing cold catches my breath.

'Hi,' he says as I approach. I stop just short of him and my whole body reaches towards everything that's about to happen.

'Hey, Jake.'

'Pretty cold.' He cups his hands and blows into them.

'Unexpected, considering the conditions,' I say, and then worry that's too snarky, but Jake just laughs and shifts against the snowmobile.

'Hey listen,' he says. 'I want to ask you something.' I say nothing, just wait. Jake reaches out one hand as if to stroke my face but instead he just tugs at the end of my hair. 'You should be wearing a beanie,' he says. 'Rach would kill me if I let her little sister get frostbite.'

'Huh?' I say. 'Rachel?'

'Yeah,' he says, and his whole face goes flabby with embarrassment. 'I wanted to ask you about her.'

'Okay,' I say, and the prickling under my armpits is back.

'Do you think she'd go out with me? If I asked her?'

The whole night swoops in and I am quiet, lost in the thick whiteness, the impossibility of this moment. I stare at the snow on Jake's scarf and watch it melt into the wool.

'Just 'cause, you know, I thought because you're her sister, you might know, or she might have mentioned me or something. Has she said anything?' He reaches to tug on my hair again. 'Huh?' He tries a goofy sort of smile. 'You think she'd be interested?'

'Um,' I say, and squint my eyes, and suddenly I'm freezing, like all my skin is icing over and beginning to crack, but there's an intense, dull heat swelling inside my ear. I can't make my mouth work because if I move all my ice-surface will splinter and then I'll just be a pile of steaming guts by the discarded skis.

'Alright?' Jake says, ruffling my hair, my perfect shiny hair which I spent so long straightening. For him.

I snatch my head away and the Snow Queen rears. I will cut off every single strand that he touched; I will hold it between the metal clamps until it burns.

Jake laughs a little, hands up, all easy. I get a whiff of garlic and my stomach shifts. 'Hey, alright. No stress. Don't worry about it.'

'I'm not,' the Snow Queen says.

Jake kicks at some snow. 'Hey, well thanks. Get back inside, yeah? It's freezing.'

He leaves, as easy as the falling snow, and I just stand there staring at nothing, at the flinty whiteness and swathe of shadows where the mountains begin. I only come around when I hear a noise and realise it's my teeth chattering.

I walk, back up the ramp and around the side of the lodge, but my body feels foreign and put together wrong. Outside of my teeth it's dead silent, the unsound draped over the ground, the trees, the roof of the lodge.

A few slobbery couples are still at the fire, but Jake isn't there. I stare at it dully and realise neither is Jesse. I walk closer to the fire, as if my little brother might be there, battling a dragon, locked in the flames.

He isn't.

Then I look around further and see his coat lying in the snow.

'Hey.' I charge at the couples, prise them apart. 'Have you seen a little kid?' They stare, slack faced. 'My brother. Did you see my brother?'

One of the guys tightens his arms around his girlfriend's waist. 'Nah man,' he says. 'Sorry. Wasn't looking.'

Heat starts to throb again at the centre of my ear. 'Jesse?' I say, running to pick up the coat. My voice sounds small and swallowed— an icicle dropping from a branch.

'You lost him?' says the guy.

'It wasn't my fault,' I shout, all Cleo now. 'I didn't even want to look after him.'

But it is my fault. I'm not in charge. I'm not in control. I'm not powerful; I can't even look after my little brother.

'Hey, he might have just gone inside,' says the guy, but I'm looking at the tracks in the snow and there's a smaller set of footprints, around where Jesse was standing. They follow my tracks for a bit, but they're all over the place, the kind a little boy might make if he was fighting dragons. At the corner of the lodge I find his discarded beanie and then the tracks veer off, towards the trees. Straight now, like Jesse's caught the scent of a dragon and taken off after it. Without a coat. Without any armour.

Five minutes. All he had to wait was five minutes. All I wanted for myself was five minutes.

I take off running after the tracks. At the beginning of the trees there's a red paper crown, sodden, torn apart, already beginning to disintegrate into the snow.

I call up the Snow Queen, I beg her to take charge. But she looks at me and her eyes are hard chips of ice. *Well everyone will notice you now.*

She flicks her wand. *Bzz,* she says to me. *Bzz,* and all I'm left holding is a flimsy paper crown.

Between Spaces

Sandy Bigna

Mum and I have been busy unpacking and all that. Trying to make this place feel like home, but I gotta say it's not feeling so much like home right now. Water drips down the walls in the stairwell. Real creepy, like you're in some horror movie and someone's about to jump out and grab you.

When we first arrived—about three weeks ago—and were hauling our bags up the steps to our apartment, these two guys were just standing about in the stairwell. Talking real quiet, hoodies pulled up, hands in pockets. As we walked past they didn't even move or anything. Just fell silent, looking at us out of the corners of their eyes. Probably planning their next robbery or something.

Well, they can try robbing us if they want, but they'll be disappointed if they do make the effort to get into our apartment, 'cause we don't have anything worth stealing.

We're using a cardboard box as a coffee table. I think that pretty much sums things up.

I wonder what you'd say about this dump of a place, Sam. You'd probably have been more chilled out about it than I am. You were always one to laugh things off or make a joke. But me, I'm about as jumpy as a cat. Every night since we got here, I lie awake and listen to all the tiny scuffling in the walls. Rats, Mum reckons, and she screws her nose up. But I don't mind. Those rats are keeping me company, I guess.

I'd rather hear the rats than the other sorts of sounds. You know what I'm talking about, Sam. The sounds that Mum and I have left behind.

Maybe I'm half-expecting Rick to come banging on our apartment door or smashing a window or something.

Maybe that's why I'm so jumpy.

***

You'd hate the smell in here though, Sam. It's that dank sort of smell. You know, like when carpet gets wet and never dries out properly. And the place is real small. There's only one bedroom, so I'm sleeping on this pull-out bed that doubles as a couch in the living area, which is also the dining room. Mum picked the bed-couch thing up from Vinnies. It's green with purple flowers on it.

Yeah, I know right. You don't need to tell me. Mum says it's really cool and retro and that look is in now. It gives me a headache. I need to wear my sunglasses whenever I look at it.

I miss my bedroom. You remember it Sam, all those band posters I blu-tacked to the wall. The Ramones and Nirvana and Metallica. And you'd remember how mean Rick got when he saw I'd used blu-tack on the wall, saying it would make the paint come off and how he didn't work two jobs just so I could damage his property and force him to spend his money fixing my mistakes.

Yeah—typical Rick stuff and I'm just glad we got away from him. That was the best day of my life when we left, but man, I hope that's the last of him.

I hope he doesn't track us down.

***

40

I miss you, Sam. I miss the way you weren't scared to sing aloud on the school bus, the way you said what you thought, the way you had a smile for everyone and a joke. You weren't the smartest kid in the class, but you were the funniest and everyone liked you, even the teachers, and sometimes they even turned a blind eye and let you wear your headphones in class.

You always had your headphones hanging around your neck. Mum said you were gonna be a rock star, and you had a way with the guitar that made her sit and listen with her eyes closed.

But mostly I think you liked playing music loud because it blocked out the sound of things smashing.

Now I don't even know where those headphones are. Everything just got shoved into boxes. We were in such a hurry to get out. Mum said we might have to leave some stuff behind—to only pack what we needed.

Just in case Rick came home early and found us packing our stuff.

It's not like the police were any help; they said they needed evidence of what was happening. And we weren't going to wait around for evidence, Mum said. She said the holes in the walls and broken things should be enough. When she said that her mouth went tight and hard and she started throwing stuff into boxes.

I thought she was going to break something.

***

Turns out Mum did break something, actually.

Today I found some smashed glass in one of the smaller boxes we hadn't got to yet. It was from a framed picture of Mum and you, when you were a baby. You had your face turned up to her, and hers was tilted down towards you and she was laughing.

Dad took that picture. Before he got sick.

I took the picture out of the frame and smoothed it out a little and put it in the cardboard box where my clothes were stashed. Mum said we'd get a wardrobe for my clothes soon, but first things first.

Things like beds were more important, she reckoned, and kitchen stuff so we could cook and eat.

'When I get a job it'll be different, you'll see,' she said, putting her arm around my shoulders.

***

I decided I'd better take the broken glass out to the dumpster before one of us got cut. Last thing we needed right now.

The dumpster was in this smelly laneway that ran alongside the apartment block. There was graffiti everywhere and the fence palings were all broken like smashed teeth.

The sun burned the back of my neck as I left the shade to dump the rubbish. I could already feel sweat starting to prickle under my arms. I shook my fringe out of my eyes. It's been a while since I've had a haircut.

I was just about to chuck the broken glass in the dumpster when a voice floated out of it: 'Watch it!'

I got such a fright I jumped backwards.

This head popped out and stared at me like I was doing something illegal by dumping stuff in the bin. Yeah, like I was the one doing something weird.

I couldn't tell if it was a boy or girl because the kid had their cap pulled down low and this husky voice, and a torn blue t-shirt with dirt stains.

'You watch it,' I retorted.

'You almost dumped that on my head.' The kid loudly chewed on some gum, still staring.

I pushed my hair out of my eyes, but it fell right back over my face like always.

'What the hell are you doing in the bin anyway?' My voice came out all rough. You would have at least managed a bit of a smile or a joke, Sam, I know you would. That's what you always did, winning people over.

But I don't have any jokes in me right now.

The kid shrugged and blew a pink bubble with the gum. 'Dumpster diving. You'd be amazed what people throw away that can be re-used. So wasteful, actually. Whatcha got in that bag?'

The kid reached for my bag and I yanked it away. The cap fell off and long straggly hair fell out from under it. So she was a girl. Who knew?

'None of ya business,' I said, meaner than necessary.

'Fine, whatever.' The girl turned away and my words hung loud between us in that still, murky laneway air

'Just some broken glass,' I muttered, softer.

The girl hoisted herself up onto the edge of the dumpster, legs dangling over the side. 'Well, go on, chuck it in then.' She blew another bubble and sat there, waiting.

I threw the bag into the dumpster where it landed with a dusty thud.

Then I just sort of stood there with my hands in my pockets. I felt myself hunching over in my too big t-shirt, trying to look less lanky.

The girl was watching me, staring, like she had no issues with what is socially acceptable. I turned to go, but then the husky voice floated towards my back: 'I found something really awesome in the dumpster across the road yesterday, actually.'

I stopped and sighed. I didn't feel like making small talk.

But you would have tried, Sam. You would have been a better person.

So I half-turned back to her. She cracked her gum, shoving her cap back over her messy hair. It looked like she cut her hair herself—all lopsided, fringe blunt and uneven—showing a high pale forehead.

'Don't you want to know what it is?'

I shrugged. 'Whatever.'

The girl obviously took that as a yes. She jumped down, wiping her hands on the side of her jeans, which I noticed now had these coloured patches stitched all over them.

She started walking, then stopped and turned back around. 'Coming?'

Hands still shoved in my pockets I followed her back towards the front of the apartment. I guess I had nothing better to do. Aside from unpacking boxes. But truthfully, I was a bit over that now.

And let's face it, nobody else around here had bothered to give me the time of day. Mum had reckoned people might be friendly, but mostly they just brushed past us in the stairwell.

***

The girl led me towards one of the apartment doors on the ground floor. She pushed the door open and I hung back. It felt a bit weird going into her apartment seeing as we'd only just met.

She stopped in the doorway and rolled her eyes. 'You just gonna hang out in the stairwell all day? Gonna admire the view?' She swept her hand out like there was some amazing artwork all around us in the dim, dank light out here. Bit of a smart mouth, this kid.

I call her a kid, but I guess she was around my age, about fourteen, maybe even a year or so older.

'Might be better than listening to your wise cracks,' I muttered.

But I followed her in and closed the door behind me, because she didn't bother.

When I turned back to the room, I let my hands drop to my sides, and I had to blink a few times as my eyes adjusted to the light after the dark stairwell.

There was so much colour in the room it was hard to breathe for a moment just looking at it all. Metal sculptures on the floor, bright-splashed paintings on the walls, coloured candles and books all over the shelves. Mobiles hanging from the ceiling threw rainbow light onto the walls. It was all so bright and warm I felt these stupid tears prick the back of my eyes.

I shoved my hands back in my pockets and took a few deep breaths. 'Damn it Tiger, don't embarrass yourself,' I muttered through gritted teeth.

The girl wasn't even looking at me anyway. Standing in the kitchen area, she yelled, 'Ange! Where'd you put that table I found yesterday?'

My breathing slowed and I looked around like it was no big deal, and the embarrassing need to cry passed.

You would never have cried, Sam, and certainly not in front of strangers. The only crying you ever did was in bed at night when you were alone, and it was a tight, soundless crying that melted into the dark.

***

I realised this apartment was the mirror image of the one Mum and I were in, but somehow the space felt lighter, airier. Guess it was all the coloured stuff everywhere. Totally not Mum's scene. She liked cool, dark colours and quiet spaces to curl into.

Guess it's 'cause she was used to hiding. Standing in this stranger's living room I got a flashback of Mum grabbing me out of bed one night and shoving me into the wardrobe in my bedroom. Then she climbed in after me and held me tight against her chest. I could hear her heart all jumpy and fast and her breathing coming out ragged and raspy, like she'd run a big marathon. We sat like that, curled into the tiny, dark space for what felt like forever. But even though the wardrobe door was closed, the shouting and smashing going on outside leapt in loud as fireworks.

I squeezed my eyes shut real quick to get rid of the memory, and when I opened them again, the person who I guessed must be Ange came into the room. She was in a wheelchair and had a knitted yellow rug over her legs. Her hair was bright red and spiky, and she had tattoos all up her arms. She sure wasn't like other people's mums.

'Quit yelling, Darcy!' she yelled back, but her tone was as cheerful as the yellow blanket. You would have felt the same way I did, Sam, finding it strange that yelling could be harmless, that it didn't always have to cut you like glass shards.

When Ange noticed me standing there in the living area her eyebrows shot up. 'Oh–hello! I haven't met you before!'

'Oh, I found him out at the dumpster,' the girl–Darcy–said, with a wave of her hand, like I was some stray dog she'd rescued.

Maybe I was a stray; I sure felt like one at that moment. Because my heart didn't have a home and it was like I was between spaces.

'Cool.' Ange seemed perfectly relaxed having some strange kid appear in her house. 'What's your name, mate?'

And Sam, that's where I hesitated. My mind went all blank and I panicked for a moment.

Who am I, who am I?

The world seemed to spin.

I blinked and everything went still again.

And there was your voice, telling me quiet and calm what to say.

'Tiger,' I said, quickly. 'My name's Tiger.'

'Is that even a name?' Darcy appeared next to Ange and they were both looking at me.

'I chose it,' I said, all defensive, before I could stop myself.

'You chose your own name?' Darcy leant against the arm of the couch, which had blankets in rainbow colours draped all over it. She chewed her gum, staring.

'It's a great name,' Ange said, putting a hand on Darcy's arm. 'Strong and … brave.'

Strong and brave. Yeah, right. If only they knew. Mum said we should change our names because we were in hiding. Trying to lie low and not draw attention to ourselves. Start afresh as new people.

I chose the name Tiger for myself because I wanted to be strong and brave, but I'm not—not really. I couldn't stop Rick hurting us and destroying things. I wasn't strong enough to stop him, although I wanted to.

Sam, you know how much I wanted to.

But in the end, I couldn't.

***

Ange reached out a hand to me. 'Good to meet you Tiger. I'm Ange. And seems you already know my dumpster-diving daughter, Darcy.'

When Ange grinned she showcased a gap where a front tooth should be. I looked away.

'Got my tooth knocked out in a bar fight,' Ange said, like she knew I was trying not to stare. 'You should see the other guy.'

I threw her a sideways glance from under my fringe, and she winked at me.

I half-smiled back. You'd have liked her, Sam. You'd have chatted to her more, in that easy way you had. You'd have made her laugh.

It's all I could do just to throw her an occasional, self-conscious smile.

I think it's from Mum telling me to lie low, not say too much to people about our background, or where we were from. It was making me edgy, fugitive-style. I just needed a long trench coat and sunnies to really get into character.

At that point, Darcy, who had briefly disappeared, yelled out from what must be the one bedroom in the apartment, 'Hey Tiger Boy, come and see!'

I shuffled my feet on the floor.

Ange gave a little nod. It was like she could see the tightness in me, the hesitation. 'It's ok, go on.'

I heard the soft run of her wheels on the floor behind me as I wandered into the room. I wouldn't trust me alone with her daughter either. My clothes hung off me because they were all too big (there wasn't heaps of choice when mum took me shopping at Vinnies), my hair was so long it hung over my eyes, and I could barely make eye contact.

Yeah, I must have looked a bit dodgy. Maybe it was best I didn't have that trench coat.

**

I stopped in the small room and looked about me, slack-jawed. So much stuff in here. There were lamps and clocks and radios and toys and chairs and computer screens and small tables. Were these guys hoarders?

'Well, what d'ya think Tiger Boy?' Darcy sounded impatient. 'This is all the stuff we've fixed up–you know, other people's trash from the dumpsters, like I told you.'

'Wow.' I cleared my throat. 'So … what do you do with all the stuff?'

Ange wheeled up alongside me. 'Some of it we keep. Some of it we sell. Brings in a little bit of pocket money, hey. You'd be amazed what people are so hasty to chuck in the bin. If they just held onto it and tinkered around a little bit they could keep on using it. But nah–most people are too lazy and just want to chuck out the old so they can buy something new. Adding to landfill.'

'Uh, yeah.' I shuffled my feet again, looking down, thinking of the stuff Mum and I had dumped over the last couple of weeks as we took stuff out of our boxes. Cupboard space here wasn't exactly roomy so Mum kept telling me to take stuff out to the trash. Some of it has probably already ended up in this room.

'This is what I found yesterday across the road – come and see!' Darcy waved me over and I edged closer to the small table she was kneeling in front of. It was a sad, old-fashioned rickety-looking table. Kinda looked like trash to me, but Darcy was running her hand over it, like some valuable treasure.

'See? Isn't it amazing?' Her quiet tone seemed odd after all her yelling and wise cracks.

''Um. Yeah,' I muttered.

'With a bit of love and care this will be a real beauty,' Ange added into the silence.

'I'm gonna take it outside now and start working on it.' Darcy stood up, rubbing her hands on her grubby jeans.

'Sure,' Ange said. 'Just be back for dinner, right?'

'Yeah, yeah.' Darcy picked up the table and started walking out of the room. 'Coming?' she said over her shoulder.

I stole a glance at Ange. She was looking at me with bright eyes and a smile.

I shrugged. 'Sure. Got nuthin' on this arvo I guess,' I added, in case they thought I was some loser with no friends.

Which is true, because we left my mates behind at the old place and here we don't know anybody. Mum said I have to start going to the local school, and I might make new friends there but it's summer holidays so that's still weeks away.

And anyway, I don't want to make new friends. The ones I already had were pretty cool. They must wonder where I am now. Sometimes I wonder if they'll go past my old house, knock on the door. That thought makes my blood rush. What will Rick say to them? Will he try to get them to tell him where we went? Lucky none of them know, because Mum made me promise not to tell anybody, not a soul.

Sam, you know I'm good at keeping secrets.

When the teachers started asking if there was anything going on at home, I kept my mouth shut, just like Mum told me to. If people started sniffing around, she said, that would make things worse. Best to just tough it out, she told me, then we'd make our great escape.

***

And now here I am, following some dumpster-diving girl back outside into the harsh bright light.

'Want me to carry the table?' I offered, as an after-thought. You would have offered sooner, Sam, you were always quick to help, you noticed when people needed a hand. That's another reason why everyone liked you so much.

But Darcy wasn't one of those people who accepted things graciously, it seemed. 'Nah. I reckon I'm stronger than you anyway,' she said.

My jaw tightened, but then she threw me this backwards grin. I relaxed a little.

The grass crunched like dry biscuits under our shoes. The tip of one sneaker had a hole in it, I noticed as I glanced down. There was this hot throbbing sound of cicadas in the trees all around us, which made the air feel even more stifling.

Darcy went around to a patch of shade under the trees, where the grass was flattened and yellowish. 'Wait here,' Darcy said, putting the table down. I watched her disappear behind the back of the apartment building. Then she came back carrying a toolbox. She put it down next to the table and knelt, touching the table with her fingertips, head slightly tilted.

I couldn't stop watching her when she did that. She was like some artist, surveying an empty canvas. Her tongue poked out a little between her top teeth. I also noticed for the first time that her eyes were different colours. One was blue—like, pure blue—and the other was brownish. How did I not notice that before? I guess I'd been avoiding eye contact.

***

Darcy looked up and I quickly looked back down at my ragged shoes, my cheeks hot. Geez, I hoped she didn't think I was checking her out or something. That stuff was so not on my radar at that point in time.

But she didn't seem to have noticed anything.

'Open the toolbox,' she instructed me.

I found myself doing what she said, like I'd lost my own sense of direction.

You wouldn't even recognise me right now, Sam. You always knew who you were and where you were going. You had a clear path.

But me right now ... there was nothing clear about my path.

I watched Darcy take out the tools she needed, and start working on that sad old table, sanding it back. The table leant to one side a little and somehow looked even sadder out here under this big expanse of sky. Small and scuff-marked and useless, like it had no purpose and nobody even knew where it came from or who it had belonged to. It looked like it had been chucked around a bit, maybe kicked at and treated like garbage.

Staring at that crappy old table, my heart gave a sudden jolt.

***

Mum was pretty annoyed when I eventually came back to the apartment. I didn't realise how much time had passed. I'd stayed out there with Darcy I guess for an hour or so, just sitting in the shade, occasionally passing tools her way. Luckily she didn't seem to care that I wasn't big on chatting.

Not like you, Sam. You used to love a chat. I still don't get how we can be so different, you and me.

Anyway, I guess it was kinda peaceful, sitting out there in the shade, not having to say too much. For the first time that tight little fist in my stomach started to unclench. Just a little.

'Come by my place tomorrow,' Darcy said in that slightly bossy tone, when I finally got up to leave. The shadows had started to lengthen across the grass.

I just shrugged and walked off.

'You'll be back,' Darcy yelled after me.

I looked down at my shoes as I walked across the crunchy grass. My toe was poking through the dirty green sock. And even though no one could see me, no one except those damn grasshoppers leaping around me like firecrackers, I ducked my head to hide the beginnings of a smile.

***

But yeah … Mum was pissed. Said she'd looked for me everywhere. The last thing she knew, I'd ducked out to throw some garbage, she said, and then three hours later I still hadn't come back. Reckoned she'd even been about to call the police. She can't have looked very hard if she didn't even think to check under the trees behind the apartment block.

'Slight overreaction,' I'd muttered, but when I saw her face I realised that was a mistake. Mum went into her bedroom and slammed the door and I sat out there in the living area/bedroom by myself feeling like a low life as shadows crept across the room like long fingers.

***

The next few days were spent hanging with Darcy, watching her working on the table. Sometimes Ange made her way out too, offering us drinks and stuff, stopping to give advice or have a quick chat.

I felt relieved that neither of them asked where I'd come from, or any questions about Mum or I. Ange joked around with us a lot, throwing us her gap-toothed smile, and sometimes I even found myself smiling back, making eye contact.

My shoulders were starting to feel looser.

***

After a few days Darcy came banging on my apartment door. Said she had something to show me. I let her drag me by the arm down stairs to her apartment. We stepped inside and there sitting in the entrance was that sad old table she'd been working on. Except it wasn't sad anymore—it had been sanded back, polished and painted a bright yellow. The legs had been straightened. It caught the light from the hanging crystals and glimmered back at me like the sun.

Darcy nudged me in the ribs. 'Well?'

And Sam, I felt my breath catch in my lungs just looking at the creaky old table now standing straight and proud and full of light.

I cleared my throat. 'Yeah. It's alright, I guess.'

'Huh.' Darcy poked me in the ribs again. 'Well, anyway, do you need me to help you to carry it back to your apartment? I know you're not real strong.'

And she threw me this sideways grin.

I stared at her. 'What?'

She shrugged, impatient. 'It's yours, dummy. You said you're using a cardboard box as a coffee table, so thought you might prefer this.'

My heart jumped. I couldn't say anything. I stood there trying to imagine this shiny yellow table as bright as a sunflower in our dingy apartment. I couldn't even say thanks.

But that was ok. I think Darcy understood.

***

I knelt in front of the table, with its clean lines shiny with hope. It somehow made the small dark space feel lighter, airier. I ran my hand gently over the polished top.

I heard Mum come up behind me. Heard her soft breathing. She put a hand on my shoulder.

'Hey. I have something to tell you.'

And Sam, I can tell you right now, my heart just flipped like a fish. I felt sick.

He'd found us. We had to pack and run. Just as I was starting to find my feet. To feel more like me. More like you, Sam.

But when I turned to look at Mum, her face was soft.

'They got him, darl. He stuffed up when he went ahead with that robbery plan with his idiot mates. He's in custody.'

My head spun. Rick was in custody.

Did that mean we didn't have to hide anymore?

Mum nodded at me gently, like she could read my mind.

She put an arm around me, kneeling in front of the table. Her other hand gently stroked it.

'We're going to be ok, Sam ... I mean, Tiger. Tiger.'

My throat felt thick with tears. I straightened my shoulders.

I'm Tiger. But I'm also Sam.

And Sam-maybe, just maybe, I can start to find a way back to you.

Perennial

Kelly Emmerton

Six days after

The day they buried John was bright and clear, with a breath of crisp wind and not a cloud in the sky.

Ben and Adam stood side-by-side on the manicured lawn, in pressed shirts and trousers usually reserved for the office as they watched him being lowered into the ground.

They hugged John's mum and shook his dad's hand. As children, his mum had healed countless scrapes and bruises for all three of them. In their teenage years, his dad had pretended not to notice them sneaking through John's window well past curfew. When the three of them moved out together and started work at the same company, his parents bought them all matching ties and laughed far too long at their own joke.

Now, John's dad looked deflated, eyes red and mouth downcast. His mum couldn't even look at them and turned away without speaking.

When all was said and done, they took the bus home to a three-bedroom flat, the sun still high and bright in the sky.

***

Nine days after

The day they came to scour the flat of John's presence, it rained all day long.

As the remains of a life were packed away in boxes and loaded into the back of a borrowed truck, Adam and Ben hovered, getting under the feet of the assortment of cousins and family friends who had volunteered for the job.

Adam stood in doorways—silent, watching—until the rooms were emptied of everything John had owned. He watched from the kitchen window as they hauled boxes out to the truck and snapped the doors shut, trying in vain to keep the rain out.

Ben flitted from room to room, person to person, trying to help, but unable to touch any of the things being packed away, as if they were cursed objects. He rung his hands and made cups of tea that went undrunk and then stood at the door as the truck disappeared down the street.

Alone again, they sat side by side on the lounge and stared at the blank TV screen. The rain went on, relentless.

***

Fifteen days after

Adam woke up slowly, confused as to what woke him, before he recognised the smell of bacon.

When he staggered out to the kitchen in his flannelette pyjama bottoms and one sock, Ben was already dressed, buzzing around the kitchen with spatula in hand, to the soundtrack of sizzling from the pan. 'Morning.'

'M'rnin'. Tea?'

'Ta.'

Adam flicked the kettle on and took down three mugs from the cupboard above it, dropping a teabag into each one. Yawning so widely his jaw cracked, he watched from the corner of his eye as Ben dished up three serves of bacon and eggs. Sunday fry-ups was an old and well-loved tradition—Adam could tell which plate was his by how well-done the eggs were and by the fact that Ben had once again gifted himself an extra rasher of bacon.

The steaming kettle clicked off and he reached for it, pouring three mugs. One with sugar, no milk; the second, milk, no sugar; and finally, plenty of milk, plenty of sugar. It was only when the teabags were in the bin that he stopped and stared at the milk and sugar concoction in the third mug. Jaw clenched and eyes turned away, he poured it down the sink and joined Ben at the table.

They both ignored the third plate of bacon and extra runny eggs abandoned by the stove top, and the empty chair between them.

***

Life went on in much the same way as it always had. They went to the pub and took turns to buy rounds of three pints. They visited the little rundown theatre down the road that only played classics in black and white and sat in the back row, either side of the centre seat. They made too much breakfast and too many mugs of tea.

Life went on. And if it was different than it was before, they didn't mention it.

***

Sixteen days after

The office was quiet, other than the low drone of a phone call from some distant cubicle and the constant hum of the copy machine.

In his cubicle, Ben tapped single computer keys in slow succession, pecking out a nonsense sentence, then deleting it letter by letter and starting again. It was 3pm. Only two hours until they could go home. That was only one hour, two times over. It was only thirty minutes four times.

His intense concentration was broken as someone he'd never seen in the office before walked past, carrying a cardboard box of office supplies. A porcelain frog with large, crossed eyes peered out the top.

Ben rolled to the door of his cubicle to watch as the intruder stepped into the cubicle next to his and then didn't come back out. Eyes wide and heart thudding, he scuttled back to his desk and scrunched a piece of paper into a ball without checking what it was.

Stepping carefully up onto his chair so his head poked above the top of the sea of cubicles, he lobbed the paper over the empty cubicle—now inhabited by the intruder—and into Adam's.

It only took a minute for Adam's head to pop up over the cubicle walls as well.

'What?' he mouthed.

Ben pointed down into the cubicle between them. Frowning, Adam looked and then jerked backward, disappearing from view with the tell-tale squeal of chair wheels across the floor.

**

They appeared side-by-side in the cubicle doorway and watched as the intruder settled the porcelain frog on the edge of the monitor, where it leered at them with bulbous, crossed eyes. The intruder looked up at them as well, breaking into a wide, crooked smile.

'Hi! I'm Herbert. The new guy.' He bounced out of the desk chair, hand extended. 'Friends call me Herb.'

A muscle in Adam's jaw twitched. Ben's fingers drummed against his thigh. For a long, drawn out moment the three men stood staring at each other. There was something building in the silence, something cold and heavy pushing its way to the surface. It bubbled up between them, threatening to spill over at any moment.

They glared silently at the intruder Herbert for a moment longer. Then, ignoring the tension, they went to lunch.

**

Twenty-seven days after

Ben stepped into the bathroom, smacking his lips and yawning. It was chilly in the early morning air and he shifted from foot to foot on the cool tiles as he positioned himself in front of the toilet.

His eyes, still heavy with sleep, slid closed. And then snapped open. He blinked once, and then again.

It was still there.

'Adam!'

***

Adam and Ben stood side by side in front of the toilet, staring at the pot plant on the windowsill. It had large, waxy green leaves and was standing proudly in a blue pot with a chip in the rim. It had been there for years. For so long, they'd stopped noticing it. Until now.

Ben cleared his throat. 'What do we do with it?'

'I don't ... I don't know.'

They stared at the plant a moment longer. It didn't move.

'Should we ... call them? To come get it?'

Adam frowned, then shook his head. 'They're not gonna come all the way over here just to get his pot plant.'

He reached out as if to pick the pot up and then stopped, hand hovering in the air. It was as if time had slowed to an unnoticeable crawl. Spine rigid, he backed away, out of the bathroom and exhaled. 'Just leave it. Don't—don't touch it.'

Ben let him go.

***

Twenty-eight days after

Adam woke slowly, to the smell of bacon.

When he shuffled out to the kitchen Ben was already dressed and standing at the stove, spatula in hand.

'Morning.'

'M'rnin'. Tea?'

'Ta.'

He flicked the kettle on and took down three mugs, dropping a teabag into each one, as Ben dished up three serves of bacon and eggs. As he slumped against the counter and waited for the kettle to boil, he came face to face with the plant.

It was sitting next to the stove, unassuming.

He stared a little longer, then looked at Ben, who studiously did not look back.

The kettle clicked off and Adam poured three mugs. Sugar, no milk; milk, no sugar; plenty of both.

When the teabags were in the bin he stopped, stared at the third mug and sighed, running a hand through his hair.

Just before he dumped it into the sink he paused, glossy green leaves catching his eye. The mug was warm. It seemed a shame to waste tea, even if it was too sweet and too milky on the whole.

He poured the tea into the soil at the top of the blue pot, and before it had soaked in all the way, he'd scooped the plant up off the counter. Taking his seat in front of a plate of runny eggs and crisp bacon, he placed the pot plant on the third empty chair.

Ben glanced at it and finally met his eye. Neither said a word.

***

Twenty-nine days after

They took the plant to work.

In the elevator, they stood with three of their co-workers, eyes ahead. When the doors opened on the floor below theirs, one man muttered 'Excuse me,' glancing sideways as he brushed past, jostling the plant's leaves.

On their floor, in the cubicle between theirs, the intruder Herbert was typing something up, every click-clack of the keyboard obnoxious. They stood shoulder to shoulder in the doorway and glared.

'Hi guys!' Herbert had caught sight of them from the corner of his eye.

With the plant cradled in is arms, Adam stepped into the cubicle. He ignored Herbert and settled the pot gently on the desk, on top of a stack of printed pages. Then he retreated and the two of them disappeared back into their own cubicles.

Herbert blinked at the plant sitting on his desk but left it there for the day. When he returned from the kitchen just before five o'clock, his washed and dried Tupperware in hand, it had vanished.

***

A round of three pints in a pub, one emptied into soil. Three tickets for a movie they'd watched a hundred times. Crispy bacon and runny eggs and tea with too much sugar and milk.

Life went on, more and more like it had always been.

***

Fifty-six days after

Adam woke up slowly, to the smell of bacon and shuffled out to the kitchen, where Ben was already dressed and standing at the stove.

'Morning.'

'M'rnin'. Tea?'

'Ta.'

He flicked the kettle on and took down three mugs, dropping a teabag into each one. Ben was humming beneath his breath as he flipped the eggs out onto plates.

Adam slumped against the counter and stared blankly at the kettle, rubbing at the stubble on his jaw.

'Adam!'

He turned slowly. It was too early for yelling.

Ben was standing at the table, hands full with their breakfasts, staring down at the plant, where it was waiting in its usual chair. When Adam came to look over his shoulder, he was jolted suddenly into wakefulness.

'What did you do to it?'

The plant was drooping and turning brown at the edges of its leaves, which were now distinctly less glossy than they'd been the night before. It looked sick and sad.

Turning on him, Ben shook his head, fast and frantic. 'I didn't touch it!' Then he frowned. 'It's probably from all the tea you've been giving it! It's too much sugar!'

'Me? You shouldn't have bought that last round—that's what's done it!'

Between them, a single leaf dropped off the plant.

Adam grabbed the pot. 'C'mon.'

***

It was a brisk, bright Sunday and the florist three blocks from their flat was busy. When they slammed through the front door, the bell above it chimed loudly with the sudden intrusion and heads turned in their direction. Neither noticed, making a beeline for the counter, where a florist in a dark green apron holding a large bunch of pink flowers watched them approach with wide eyes.

'Please, we need your help!'

The florist turned fully to them, a tiny frown puckering her lips. She glanced at the door, as if expecting to see someone chasing them.

'You have to fix our plant!' Adam thrust the pot plant onto the counter and the force of it made another leaf drop from its place. They exchanged panicked glances.

The florist, laying her bunch of flowers gently down on a side bench, looked at the plant, and then back up at them.

'Well?' Ben prompted. 'Do something!'

She lifted one of the drooping, browning leaves with a single finger, then let it flop back down again.

She shook her head. 'I can't.'

'What?!'

'No! You have to! It's dying!'

'It was fine yesterday!'

'Nothing was wrong!'

'We thought he was happy!'

Ben and Adam froze and very carefully did not look at each other.

The florist raised her hands as if to stop them going any further. She needn't have bothered—both had found their mouths were suddenly dry, words trapped behind their teeth.

'Listen, boys, I can't do anything —' the florist raised her hands a little more, expecting an onslaught of protest '—because there's nothing wrong with this plant. It's a perennial. It will die off and bloom each year.'

Adam and Ben stared at her, mouths open.

She shrugged. 'It's doing exactly what it's supposed to.'

***

There was a chilly breeze whipping through the park. Ben and Adam huddled at opposite ends of a bench, hugging themselves against the cold. Between them, the drooping plant dropped another leaf. Neither of them looked at it.

A woman in spandex shorts jogged past and looked a little too long at Adam's pyjama bottoms and chest, clearly bare beneath his denim jacket. He didn't notice her mildly alarmed gaze, too caught up in his own thoughts.

It was a long time before he marshalled them well enough to share. 'Perennial. What the hell?'

He paused, jamming his cold hands beneath his arms. 'Do you think that lady was really a florist? Who's ever heard of a perennial bloody pot plant?'

He paused again, and when Ben didn't reply, 'Did you ever see it do that before?'

'No.' Ben hesitated. 'Do you think we should have known?'

The question dropped between them like a stone in a still pool. Adam shifted in his seat. 'How could we have?'

They fell silent again. The breeze rustled the trees and Adam tugged his jacket tighter around him.

Another leaf fell from the pot plant.

Ben swallowed hard. 'Do you think he ever told us?'

They stared straight ahead.

Slowly, Adam leant forward, dropping his head into his hands. 'He was fine.'

'Obviously he wasn't.'

And then, like a rubber band snapping, Ben began to cry. Adam dragged in a shaky breath and then leant over to grip his shoulder. Ben grabbed his hand and squeezed.

They sat for a moment with nothing but the shedding pot plant and their own wet breathing as company. Then Ben sniffed loudly, wiped his face, and straightened up.

'Are we fine?' he asked.

Adam sighed, squeezed his shoulder, and let go. 'Yeah. Yeah I think we will be.'

Uplifted

Frances Prentice

Bare feet digging into warm sand, the tangy taste of salt air, man-sized kites skimming the dunes. My heart soared with my father and his friends as they climbed higher and higher into the blue skies, skillfully cruising up and down the coastline. Dad alighted on the narrow beach, running briefly before lowering the nose of his glider into the soft sand. He grinned broadly as he greeted me, his six-year-old sand-covered princess, unclipping his harness from the A-frame so I could bundle it into my arms and carry it back up the slope, while he shouldered the now cumbersome craft to ascend the dune, ready to launch again. Back then, I was his mate, and he was my world.

I remember the day I stepped down from the bus from high school, surprised to see Dad at the stop. I grinned and waved at him, anticipating an afternoon of surfing. Dad had begun teaching me the previous year, but wasn't often home early enough to go to the beach after school. Matt was beside him, jumping up and down.

'Hey, Su-su, guess what?'

'No idea, short stuff!' I rubbed his spikey hair.

'We get to live in the country and Dad says maybe I can have a motorbike. Brmmmm!' He raced ahead of us, his hands revving the imaginary throttle of a Pee-Wee 50.

'Dad?' A lump in my throat prevented me saying more.

Dad looked at me, and I could see the mixed emotions in his eyes. I guess he knew I'd be upset. 'Sorry, Sukie, I didn't want to tell you 'til I was sure. I got a position as a manager at a small motors shop in a country town. It's a step-up for me. It'll just be for a few years.'

'A few years?' Tears welled in my eyes and I ran into the house, slipping past Mum and heading for the security of my bedroom. Arms around my favourite cushion I rocked there, listening to the comforting roar of the waves. I had heard what Dad said, but I still didn't understand. Why couldn't he have found a promotion closer? How could he want to leave the familiarity of the dunes and the soaring gulls? I'd thought he loved our coastal home, as I did.

Our new home was surrounded by rolling hills, grassed slopes clipped short by cows and sheep. Dad purchased an ancient Land Rover, slapping on a couple of pots of green house paint, with brown trim. My mother became the chauffeur, gamely driving down steep, rutted tracks on the hills of accommodating farmers. My younger brother manned the CB radio, talking to Dad over the scratchy airwaves as they craned their heads out the windows trying to spot his red and white hang-glider in the skies above. I watched eagles soaring with my father. My feelings were mixed. I longed to be up there with them, with him, a bird among the birds.

At home, Dad never knew of this dream of mine. I had turned cold towards him, answering questions with monosyllables, if I answered him at all. It seemed I could not forgive him from dragging me away from the home I loved, the friends with whom I had begun school. Texting, emails, none if it was the same as seeing them all every day. I had nothing in common with the country kids at the local high school—football games and trail bike riding were foreign to me, and they had no interest in the surfing or lifesaving training that I'd begun just before we'd been wrenched away. The gap continually widened between Dad and I; he retreated before my stony glare.

Over breakfast one Friday morning, Dad caught my eye.

'Sukie …' I flinched at his baby name for me. He began again, clearing his throat, 'Susan, have you heard me talk about Mike, the new mechanic at work?'

I looked intently at my stubby, bitten nails, wondering where this was leading.

Dad, used to my unresponsiveness, ploughed on. 'Well, I was telling him about hang-gliding, and he said he'd like to have a go. I wouldn't mind giving him a day's training, but I really need another pair of hands …'

I looked up as he paused, and he launched back in, 'Well, I've noticed you've shot up a lot recently—you'd be tall enough to help on the wing, and strong enough to have a go now if you want to.' He finished with a rush, then took a mouthful of cereal, trying hard to seem like he didn't care too much one way or the other.

My stomach churned and my filled spoon returned to the bowl. Would I? Would I like to try flying? In my mind's eye I was an eagle, soaring, weightless in the cool air.

The silence in the kitchen expanded until we seemed as far away from each other as the clouds above the earth. Was it possible to cross such a wide expanse? Could I do it? I knew this was Dad's way of reaching out. Would I move towards him, or allow my resentment to keep us apart? I didn't know what I would say, until the words came out my mouth:

'Alright, if you want.'

'Tomorrow? We'll have to get up early before the day gets too hot.'

I nodded, still avoiding his eye. Was this really a good idea? I didn't know how to be with my dad anymore. My stomach was churning but I kept eating, and so did Dad, the sound of our chinking spoons and chewing unnaturally loud. I scraped my bowl clean, dumping it in the sink and escaping as soon as I could. Glancing back at Dad as I left the kitchen, I saw him heave a sigh. Perhaps this had been as tough on him as it had been on me.

We arrived at the paddock just as the sun was stretching out its rays over the rolling hills behind the training slope. It seemed a long time since I had been up this early; a long time since I'd communed with the sun.

Dad's voice cut through my thoughts. 'Get those straps off, will you, Sukie?' He flung the words over his shoulder as he strode over to the gate to open it for Mike, who had just pulled up.

I fumbled with the straps holding the glider on the roof bars, tugging hard to release them, determined to prove that I was capable. I had just collected the final one and was bundling them into the backseat when Dad and Mike came over. Dad nodded at me, then balanced on the sidestep so he could roll the zippered hang-glider onto his shoulder and carry it to the top of a short slope. Before long, we were dragging the familiar wings out into position. Mike watched in awe as I went through the procedure with Dad, lost in a haze of memories. I could almost feel the warm sand under my bare feet, and see my childish hands and hear my chatter as we worked. My still tongue felt strange as we worked through the process efficiently: king post up, batons slotted into their narrow pockets and clipped in place. As we erected the A-frame, the wires became taut. Suddenly, it was no longer sailcloth and aluminum, it was the eager body of a bird perched, ready to fly.

Dad clipped the harness in place. 'Let's do a hang-check, Sukie.'

Mike looked baffled, but I knew what he meant. I moved forward to the harness and wriggled my way into it, then lay down so Dad could check that it was all connected correctly and the nuts and bolts were all safely fastened. It was strange to be back in the familiar rough red material. It fit me now—when I had hung in it as a child it would envelop me like a warm, red cave. I felt as if I had returned to my roots, and I was reluctant to climb out again.

Dad shouldered the glider easily. 'Stand back now, you two,' he instructed, glancing at us on either side. 'See you at the bottom!' He ran forward and the hang-glider rose into the air, skimming over the rough ground. Mike and I ran alongside, craning our heads to watch him, then catching the side wires as he landed.

'Short and sweet,' he said with a broad smile. 'Who's up next?'

'I will, if that's alright?' Mike looked at me. I felt torn, longing to be the next to launch, but not wanting to seem too eager. I shrugged, and Dad nodded to Mike.

'Okay, then, let's get this bird back to the take-off.' Dad carried the A-frame, with the nose tilted backwards behind him, and Mike and I held onto the side wires to help him keep it level as we carried it back up the slope.

Dad instructed him as I held the nose wires, then we both held onto the wires on the wing tips and ran down the slope; I was leaping with my arm stretched high above my head, as the wind pulled the glider into the air. Mike whooped and I felt my mouth curve into a smile. Dad grinned at me, his eyes twinkling.

Soon, it was Mike's turn to hold the wires. I slipped on the helmet he handed me, then stepped into the harness once more, laying down to dangle like a pendulum for the hang check before standing up again. Dad helped me lift the heavy glider. I wrapped my arms around the A-frame and balanced it on my shoulders, just as I'd seen him do a thousand times. Then, as Mike moved to the wing tip, Dad held the front wires and gently turned the nose of the glider, so it was pointing directly into wind. He nodded at me and I felt the wind lift the kite, allowing me to change my grip so I was lightly holding it with my hands, my wings straining in anticipation of flight.

'Just hold it steady!' he cautioned, as he moved to the other wing. 'Now run!'

I pushed off with my toes, pumping my legs like pistons across the ground, hearing the thumping feet of the men on either side. Then, suddenly, I was literally walking on air. The ground dropped away below me, and I was flying. A lightness filled me, and the shell that had enclosed my heart was shattered into a thousand pieces. I could feel it beating again, just as it had when I had lain on the beach watching my father soar above me. A few short seconds seemed a lifetime, and then my feet were on the ground once more.

Dad released me from the harness, and I turned and hugged him, my helmet bumping on his shoulder. He held me tight as tears streamed down my face. 'Happy tears?' he asked quietly, rubbing my back.

'Happy tears,' I confirmed, looking up at him.

'Shall we go again?'

Haunted

Niko Campbell-Ellis

I'm a ghost at my brother's funeral. Whenever my mother looks my way, her gaze goes straight through me. I wonder if she sees nothing at all or, worse still, if she sees right inside me. Sees the truth of what I've done.

I've only been to one funeral before, my grandad's. Old people funerals are okay, I mean, they're sad and everything but it's an okay type of sadness. At Grandad's funeral I felt sad because I was remembering the good times we had together, places he'd shown me, milkshakes we'd shared. I was sad for me because I was going to miss him. I was never sad for him. He was old and sick. For him I was glad.

That's not how it is with Billy. Everything in this generic, sorry-for-your-loss funeral house, with its budget flower arrangements and attendants in sombre charcoal suits, who look like estate agents on a side hustle, is so god-awful that sad doesn't even touch the sides. Billy has been with me for my entire life and I've never had to imagine a world without him. For Mum—in fact, for every other person here—there's been a time in their life when Billy wasn't alive or they didn't know him. They know they can live without him. Not me though.

My brother has always been there. Always. But now he's gone and it's my fault.

I can't tell Mum it's my fault though. When Billy died, it was like I was erased. I could walk into the room and talk to her but she wouldn't even notice—she'd just sit there, staring at nothing. If I tell her, she'll never look at me again.

We're sitting side by side and thank god the service is nearly over. I don't know why there's so much religious stuff. "Let us all pray ... we will now listen to a hymn ..." Billy didn't believe in God but I guess when a kid dies, no one knows what to say so they fall back on tried and tested bullshit. I swear, if anyone tells me Billy is in a better place, I'll punch them in the face.

Mum's sitting so still. She looks hollow, like there is nothing of her but sadness. No blood, no beating heart. I think about holding her hand, but if she wanted that sort of comfort she would have touched me before now. I don't want to upset her any further.

After the service, we shuffle into the tearoom, which is as generic and dismal as the chapel, where we drink horrid coffee and act polite. Billy's friends mostly keep away. Lots of other people come up to me though. There are too many unsolicited shoulder touches and murmurs of "I'm so sorry." A couple of people hug me. Somebody kisses my cheek. I don't feel any of it. It's as if I've died too. One of his teachers tells me Billy has gone to a better place. I resist the urge to punch her in the face.

I look at Mum to see how she's managing. She's looking in my direction, but not at me. Of course not at me. Surrounded by people who want her to acknowledge their grief, she's clutching her teacup like a life raft. I wonder if it would be easier if I was at her side fending off some of those mourners, but unlike them, I don't want to push my grief on her.

There's a narrow veranda off the back of the tearoom, I go out there to get some air and escape all the miserable faces for a few minutes. I slide down the wall until I can rest my head on my knees. My mind is playing a warped director's cut of the past three days. Nothing good to see but it won't stop playing. Billy and Mum fighting. My last conversation with him. That knock on the door and two cops standing on our doorstep. Knowing but not knowing why they were there. Mum knowing instantly. Trying to catch her as she fell. Mum screaming and lashing out. Nails raking my skin as she clawed away from me. The ride in the police car.

The door from the tearoom opens and even though I want to be alone, I'm grateful for a reprieve from the pictures in my head. My gratitude only lasts a second though. It's Leah, Billy's girlfriend, and in my less charitable moments I have wondered if she's loving the drama of this. She slides down the wall beside me and I expect more protestations of 'I loved him, you know. I still do. I can't believe he's gone,' but we sit in silence and it's actually kind of comforting.

But the weight of my guilt gets heavier and heavier and I know if I don't leave, I'll tell Leah what I did. The words are boiling inside me; if she looked at my face she could probably read it all, printed on my skin. I want to tell her, or someone, but I can't. I'll never be able to. For the rest of my life it'll be here inside me. So I squeeze Leah's hand—which for me is pretty intimate—and go back into the hall.

Slowly everyone leaves. I'd hoped Mum and I could slink out early but of course we can't. I have no idea why you are supposed to act polite when all you want to do is howl at the moon.

When we finally get to the car, Mum must be wrecked because she lets me drive. I take the long way home because I'm not ready to drive past the spot and I know Mum isn't either. Maybe one day we'll be able to drive down that road without even thinking of Billy, but for now all I can see is his car crumpled against that tree.

Eventually we make it home. My mouth is furry with the taste of curried egg and I can't face the thought of more food, but I sit in the kitchen and encourage Mum to eat. She chews on toast, each morsel taking minutes to swallow, and looks at me for the first time all day.

'I just can't understand how it happened,' she whispers.

'Are you kidding?' I spit. Am I supposed to sit here and pretend it was an accident? Is that the only way I can get my mother to see me—if I join her in this charade? It's not worth it. I might not be ready to tell her what I did but I'm not willing to go along with this lie to get her attention.

'It happened because he made it happen,' I said, looking into her wet eyes. 'Billy killed himself.'

I expect her to slap me but she doesn't. She turns her head away and I can tell from her shoulders that she's crying again.

'You're wrong,' she whispers, so softly I can barely hear her. 'It was an accident. A horrible, horrible accident.'

'An accident?' Should I give her this, let her believe this fantasy if it will give her some comfort? But I'm drowning in guilt and outright lying doesn't feel like the way to make it better. I keep wondering what story Billy would want told, but whenever my thoughts head down that path I have to reign them in because I know he'd blame me. He'd stand up in front of everyone, point his finger at me and say, 'It's Connie's fault.'

'What sort of accident makes him run off the road, on a corner he's driven around a thousand times, into the only tree there?' I ask Mum. 'What sort of accident has him going as fast as the cops said when his license limits him to ninety?'

'Driving too fast doesn't mean it was …'

She can't even bring herself to say it.

'Yes Mum, it was. It was suicide.'

Finally she slaps me. Her hand hits my cheek with such a loud smack it ricochets inside my head. She has never hit me before. Her hands have always been safe. Tears fill my eyes, but I hold them in.

I touch my own hand to my face and breathe. I won't let her see me cry from this. I swallow it down. 'Great, thanks a lot. Mother of the year.' I stalk outside, ignoring her standing there with one hand cradled in the other, her eyes wide and staring like a shell-shocked soldier. I slam the door so hard the house whimpers.

The movie in my head is on fast forward, images flashing through my brain so fast I want to throw up. Glass on the ground. Blood on the windscreen. Vomit in my mouth. Then the hospital. White hallways. Fluorescent lights. Disinfectant smell masking the presence of death.

I can't bear to sit still and watch this hateful show so I start walking. It doesn't help and neither does jogging. But flat out running, mad-girl flight in the dark—that helps.

I run and run and run. I'm paying attention to nothing but the throbbing in my chest, the taste of blood in my mouth; the pain in my knees, ankles, legs. It's good. For the first time in three days, I don't think about Billy or death or guilt. I'm just a beating heart, pumping legs, blood, spit, burn, and glorious, blinding pain.

Eventually though, I have to stop. I spit up bile and fall onto the damp grass, panting. When I can breathe properly again the guilt kicks in. The stuff about Billy never really leaves but it dawns on me that I'm a long way from home with no phone. Mum is either completely oblivious to my absence or freaking out right now. She's probably oblivious—I mean, she's barely spoken two words to me since Thursday but part of me thinks she might be freaking out. Even though I feel guilty as hell to put her through more worry, I half-hope she has noticed I've gone.

Walking home hurts. My t-shirt is wet with sweat so even though I'm wearing a jumper I'm cold. Every joint in my body is complaining about my decision to run, but it doesn't hurt enough to stop the memories. I'm too tired to fight so I surrender to it. I remember so many stupid tiny details. The shade of orange vinyl on the chair where I waited while Mum viewed Billy's body. The way cubes of broken glass reflected sunlight like diamonds. Listening to Mum make phone calls she'd have given anything to avoid making. I remember worrying about how to write the updates on Billy's social media accounts, as if choosing the right words could make any difference at all.

Our house is lit up. Mum must have turned on every light in the place. I fantasise that she'll come running out of the house, tears streaming down her face and pull me into a hug. That she'll whisper she was scared to lose me and she's glad I'm home and she loves me.

It takes so long to walk that final few hundred metres. I'm so sore and tired, all I want to do is go to bed but I'm not that lucky. As my sneakers crunch on the gravel in our driveway, Mum comes flying out the door, spitting vitriol like an ice addict. She jabs her finger at my face, hissing words that run together, with only a few making it through to my brain. They stick though. How dare you... self-obsessed... uncaring bitch. I know she's right but I cover my ears with my hands and squeeze my eyes shut, trying to block her out. She grabs my arm, wrenching my hand from my ear and orders me inside. I pull away. She shouts at me to get inside, shoving me towards the house. My blood starts pumping again, my legs know what to do and I push past her, away from the house. She stands frozen for a moment then chases me down the driveway and grabs my jumper, but I swing round and scream, 'Don't touch me!' I rip my top out of her fingers and walk on. She tries again but I twist away from her lunging grab and hiss at her in the same voice she used on me seconds ago, 'I said don't touch me.'

'Don't you dare leave,' she shouts.

I don't even bother replying, I just walk away. I pull my hands inside my sleeves against the cold and trudge down the road. I wonder if she knows. Maybe that's why she was such a bitch. A car drives past, illuminating the empty road before me. Maybe I should go and sleep in someone's barn. When the car lights disappear in the distance, the darkness of the night swallows me whole.

Light from behind tells me another car is approaching. When I hear it, I can tell it's slowing down. The car crawls up alongside and a man's voice reaches across from the driver's side. 'Need a lift, sweetheart?'

Of course, I've been told for as long as I can remember not to accept rides from strangers. Apparently, it's not safe. But then your home and family are supposed to be safe, and you're supposed to be safe for them too, so what the hell. Anyway, it's got to be better than walking. I nod at the guy and he leans across to open the door. I'm greeted by a waft of stale cigarette smell but I ignore it. 'Hop in then.'

He doesn't ask me where I want to go, just brings his car up to speed and cruises through the night. I look out the side window at the black and grey world sliding by, then glance at the man. He's oldish, older than Mum. It's weird that he picked me up but then, if I was driving along and saw a sixteen-year-old girl walking alone in the night, I might see if she wanted a lift somewhere. There's no way to tell by looking if he's a creep or a nice guy trying to be helpful. If Billy was still alive I could have called him. He always sided with me when I fought with Mum. But I let him down, so wishing I could call him is one of my punishments. He will never come for me again.

I jump when the man grabs my thigh. I didn't even see him reach out in the dark car. His hand is hot, its heat leaches into my skin through my jeans. I try to pull away but he grips my flesh with hard fingers. He's driving faster now, one hand on the wheel. The night is raging past. I try to remember what to do in situations like this but my mind has narrowed to the sensation of hot, hard fingers digging into my leg.

He releases me for a moment, both hands on the wheel as we turn off onto another road. I don't even know where we are. I think about opening the door and jumping out but the moment is gone before I've fully thought it and his hand is back on my leg, higher this time.

'I don't want to do anything with you,' I whisper. I want to sound strong and assertive but I'm whimpering.

He doesn't answer. I wish Billy was here.

We turn onto another road, but he doesn't let me go this time. I'm lost. I wonder if Mum is going to have to bury me too, or if there'll be billboards with a photo of me and the caption; 'Have you seen Constance?' For a moment, I get distracted worrying about which photo they should use. One where my hair looks cute rather than messy, which is a fine line I so often find myself on the wrong side of since getting a pixie cut. It's a shame they wouldn't use one from some special event where I'm made up and wearing a dress because I never dress like that normally, even though I look good in some photos from our Year Ten formal last year. Then I remember what I should be worrying about. Is this man going to rape me?

He turns off the road onto a gravel driveway and pulls to a stop before a gate. The lights shine through the bars of the gate, down a straight lane to a weatherboard house, just like a hundred others in this area. There are no lights on in the house.

'You get the gate.'

It's the first time he's spoken since I got in the car and I fumble with the door handle to get out. What should I do? Is it safer to comply and hope he doesn't hurt me too badly, or make a run for it? If I run he'll chase me and can I afford to risk making him angry? And he knows where he is, I bet this place belongs to him and he knows exactly how hard it would be for me to escape. I have no idea where I am. He knows that too. He's confident I've got nowhere to go so I'll open the gate and come back to him.

My legs are reluctant to work as I shut the door and walk to the front of the car. The headlights hurt my eyes. I know I don't want to get back in the car but maybe running is more dangerous. What does he want to do that he can't do in the car? What's worth the risk of letting me out? Or if he knows how trapped I already am, maybe for him there is no risk. My fingers are shaking so much I can't open the gate latch. What should I do? I wish I believed in life after death so I could ask Billy for guidance. Not that I have to believe—I know he'd tell me to run. Billy was a flight or fight kinda guy, I can't ever imagine him laying back and taking it.

Shit. I listen to my fingers and stop fiddling with the latch. I climb the gate and jump over, stumbling but I'm up and running. There's no moon and the ground is uneven, I'm running and stumbling at an angle away from the house and the car. There's something black ahead that I hope is a patch of bush where I can hide. I hear the car door slam. Any second now he'll open the gate and chase me with the car. There's no way I can make the dark bit before then.

'Aaagh!' The yell lurches out of me as I smash into a fence. I'm tangled in wire that's caught my jumper and jeans in its barbs. Light from the car shines into the paddock off to my right. He's through the gate. I rip myself from the barbed wire and push through the fence, tearing through my jeans and leg as I pull free. I thought adrenaline is supposed to make you immune to pain but it's not working.

As fast as I can, I run towards the dark. The ground has started to slope down; I'm hoping it's a forested gully. I don't have a plan but if I can get there it'll be a start. The lights from the car are moving now, not towards me, but maybe heading for a gate. He could still beat me to the gully.

The car's headlights make running more difficult. What little light there is throws weird shadows, making me duck and weave. I blunder into another fence, tearing more shreds from my clothes and palms. I run on, downhill, for the shelter of the trees.

The headlights swing as the car bounces over rough ground but they still haven't lit me up. I hope he doesn't know where I am but it's possible he's seen and is following at a comfortable distance. Maybe this is a sick game of cat and mouse.

There's another fence at the edge of the gully but this time I slip through, barely scratching myself, and I'm among the trees.

The headlights swing across and for a moment I'm caught in the light. It was just a moment though, and with all the trees he might not have seen me. It's harder to move now; it's even darker under the canopy and the ground a minefield of holes and fallen logs. I'm scrabbling forwards, sliding my feet along the ground to find any low obstacles, arms outstretched to find higher ones.

Maybe I should stop running. That guy is probably so angry he'll kill me if he catches me. At least then it'll all be over.

But something in me won't stop running. I reach the bottom of the gully. There's a creek. The water is freezing but I wade in. I stumble and crawl along the creek bed, listening for the man.

When I hear him, he's not where I expected. I can't tell exactly, but I think he's close, almost directly up the hill from me.

'Hey sweetheart,' he taunts. I should have known when he first called me sweetheart that he was a creep. 'I know where you are and I'm going to get you.'

A light shines down to where I am and I drop into the water. So cold. The light isn't powerful—maybe just his phone torch. I watch the beam pan across the gully, sweeping past me twice more. Does that mean he doesn't know exactly where I am? I keep moving.

The torch light starts to wave wildly about. Is he coming down? I hear a thud, followed by swearing. He must have hit a tree.

The torchlight swings away. I hear him say the sweetest words and I almost cry in gratitude: 'You're too ugly anyway. I hope you get hypothermia and die. Bitch.'

I crawl out of the water and wait, shivering in the darkness, listening to him climb back up the hill. I listen to the car door slam and the engine start. I listen to him drive back down the track. The night is so quiet I hear him turn onto the other road, then onto the main road. I listen until I can't hear him anymore.

I need to get moving because if I'm still here in the daylight he might come back. I'm so cold and there isn't a part of me that doesn't hurt but I force myself to crawl up the hill, feeling my way. As I emerge from the trees into the paddock, the dark is still heavy, but I can see the stars.

I try to get my bearings. I think the gate he told me to open is over to my right, which would mean the main road should be roughly ahead. I shuffle, arms outstretched, ready to collect a fence before my face does. I probably look like a zombie.

Zombie. That fits. I feel undead. Billy is dead, fully dead, and everyone knows it. Other people like Leah are so alive it's insulting. But I'm undead. I look alive, but I'm dead inside.

I hear a car and see lights in the distance. I drop into the grass. Is it the man? The lights smudge the night then disappear, leaving the world darker than before.

I uncurl from the grass and keep shuffling. I was right about the direction of the road and once I find it, I'll be able to find my way home.

Home.

Do I even have one now?

I refuse five lifts on the walk home. I walk through darkness that fades to light. I walk through pain and hunger, fear and guilt. I walk and walk.

Mum sees me as I walk up the road towards our house. She doesn't scream but she doesn't hold me close either. She takes me by the arm, her grip as tight as her jaw, and steers me into the house.

She doesn't speak. Doesn't ask why I am bloody and tattered and dragging myself home at seven in the morning. I'm not even sure she notices. I'm fairly sure she doesn't care.

She lets go of my arm and I fall into one of the kitchen chairs, ready to take whatever she wants to throw at me. But she still doesn't scream or hit or throw things. She scrapes a chair across the tiles and sits facing me, so close our knees are touching. She looks at me. It's disturbing after all the ignoring she's done lately. I try to meet her gaze but there's something about her face, her eyes, that make me look away. Shame, guilt, embarrassment, I don't know—probably all of the above. I look at our knees instead.

'I'm sorry,' she says. So quiet, more thought than vocalisation, a whisper on the outbreath.

I look up, meet her wet eyes. 'Why?'

She takes a deep breath and lets it out slowly through partly closed lips. I've seen her do this my entire life: this is how she steadies herself. I wonder if every little thing in her life now will require this level of control.

After a long silence she starts speaking, sounding robotic. 'I'm sorry that Billy killed himself.'

'What?' I can't hide my shock. She's spent the last three days insisting Billy's death was an accident and now she's apologising for his suicide.

'I know he killed himself and I know it was because of me.'

'Oh Mum,' I grab her knees, 'that's crazy.' And it is crazy. I know for a fact that it's not her fault.

She just shakes her head and starts talking about the fight they had before he killed himself. It was a stupid fight, just like they usually were. Billy wanted to go out and Mum said he couldn't until he'd finished his English assignment. That's it really. So completely mundane. I can't believe Mum wants to blame herself because of that one little fight. She and Billy argued about crap like that all the time.

'It's not your fault,' I begin, working my way up to a confession, but she interrupts, repeats the story of their fight.

82

I try again, rushing to get my words out before she cuts me off: 'It's not your fault, it's mine. I could have stopped him, but I didn't.'

That shuts her up. She stares at me like I'm a stranger to her.

'What do you mean?'

It's harder than I expected, putting it into words, 'After Billy argued with you, he came into my room.' She nods at me to go on, not giving any space for wimping out.

'He said,' my eyes roll up to the ceiling. I watch as Billy comes into my room, indignant at Mum's unreasonableness, pacing up and down in the little space between my bed and desk. I drag my eyes back down to Mum, still sitting there, waiting to be let off her own hook.

I try again, 'He said …' I pause. I don't want to relive the last words my brother said to me and I never want to think again the last words I said to him. My nails are digging into my palms and I shove my balled fists against my forehead, hiding my face. This was a stupid idea.

'Connie,' Mum whispers, pleading for the truth. She's so hungry for a different version of events and I know I have to tell her because otherwise, she'll go on for the rest of her life living with guilt that's mine to carry.

'He told me that …' He'd paced and ranted in my room, cursing Mum, school, Leah, friends, and enemies. 'That … he couldn't take it anymore.'

I look up to see how Mum copes with this, it's bad but I know there's worse to come and I don't know if she's strong enough to hear it. She nods again, wanting me to continue.

'He said that …'—I remember the strangled voice he used when he said it too—'… he said that he hated his life and if I didn't come for a drive with him …'

I remember how angry I'd felt when he said that, how I'd wanted to tell him to piss off and sort his own shit out and that I wasn't responsible for his decisions, that I had things I needed to do and asking me to go for a drive was asking me to get in trouble too. I can't believe I was worried about getting in trouble.

I look at Mum, big eyes in a grim face, and finish in a rush: 'If I didn't come for a drive with him, he'd know that even his sister didn't give a shit about him and he might as well kill himself.'

There's no stopping the images in my head now. Telling Billy that not wanting to go for a drive didn't mean that I didn't care about him but I was sick of him threatening to kill himself.

Turning back to my homework. Billy spitting out the words, 'Thanks a lot,' as he left. Angry, but not worried, as I heard his car leave the driveway with a spray of gravel.

I don't know what Mum will do to me now she has the truth but there is no more fight left in me. If she hits me, I'll take it. If she kicks me out, I'll go.

She doesn't though. She just sits in silence, looking in my direction but with eyes so glazed it's impossible to tell if she is seeing anything at all. After a long time, I go to bed.

When I wake up I don't know what day it is. I can feel a warm body alongside my own. I turn and see Mum looking at me. We stare at each other.

'It's not your fault either,' she says after a long silence.

'I could have stopped him.'

Tears are leaking out of her eyes and soaking into the pillow and I can feel salty tracks down my own face too.

'Yes, you could have,' she says, 'And I could have too. You didn't and I didn't and we both have to live with that.'

Secret even from myself, I've been hoping Mum would say something to absolve me of guilt, show me how it could all be seen in a different light. But no.

'But it's still not your fault,' she continues, 'You didn't make him do it. He made his own decision and I'm so angry with him for that. But it was his and his alone to make. If I could turn back time

I would, if I could take his place I would … but I can't.'

'I don't know how to be without him,' I admit. I've been holding this inside, this worry that without Billy as a landmark in my life, I won't be able to find my way home.

She doesn't say anything but I can tell by the way she nods that she feels the same way. She had Billy when she was only nineteen. There's a picture of her, standing in a garden, holding him up to the camera when he was only a few days old. She is so young and so proud, her smile is a lot like Billy's when he was at his very best. She probably doesn't know how to be without him either.

So many things have happened in the last few days. Lifetimes squeezed into moments. I open my mouth to tell her I'm still angry that she hit me. I close it then open it again to tell her how close she came to losing me too, how I took a stupid risk and some guy... I close it and open again to say how scared I was when she turned cold and hard on me when she was everything I needed. I close it again. None of those things need to be said right now. I will say them, but not yet.

I put my arms around her.

'I miss him.'

'Me too,' she says.

Morning sun is coming in through my blinds, painting my room with soft light. Even though it can't change a thing, we hold on to each other.

Almost

Carla Fitzgerald

The problem with willing time to pass, is that it only works if you stop doing it. Which is why Hazel was crocheting a yellow shawl in the sitting room and not looking out the window to see if the postman was on his way up. But the bell from his bike kept distracting her. The jaunty ding drew her focus over and over. And her mother peering out the window with hope in her eyes wasn't helping either.

***

Ethan swung his backpack over his shoulder and held back as the other kids piled out of the classroom. He shifted his weight from one foot to the other and tried not to be carried along in the swell. Mila was one of the last out and surrounded by the usual impenetrable army. Today though, he couldn't help but notice, she also held back.

'So yeah, probably won't see you for a while,' he said, as the chatter faded.

'Yeah, guess not.' Mila answered.

'Do you have your own phone yet?' The words were out of his mouth before he could stop them. Hopefully, it didn't sound too eager.

'Nah, Mum said maybe, if Dad gets the night job at Coles in Wagga …' She rubbed the sole of her boot against the gravel. 'But she'd have to get one for all the kids …'

He smiled. Mila often talked about the madhouse she lived in. He thought it sounded kind of cool having all those siblings. You'd never be lonely. Although when he occasionally spotted her younger twin brothers throwing rocks at passing cars with the other Year Eight boys, he could understand the drawbacks.

'And Insta, Snapchat, still instruments of oppression, are they?'

She laughed, which was a relief. He didn't want her to think his teasing was anything other than good-natured. That she refused to conform like the girls she hung out with was one of the reasons he liked her. It was just a bit … inconvenient at times like this. And he did wonder if her principles would be tested if her family could afford *Apple* merch.

'The school is lending us a laptop to share so I should be able to use that sometime. If the internet works.' Her eyes grew wide. 'To email?'

'Oh. Okay. Sure. Email.' Dread slithered around his stomach.

'Okay.' Mila glanced over at the bus line.

It was hard to know what sort of goodbye he should give her, given that the status of their relationship was as unclear as the length of time they would be apart. His eyes flicked over to her friends waiting at the bus stop. They were laughing at something on one of their phones and making not-so-subtle faces at her.

'Okay. Seeya.' The pressure of this sudden goodbye swelled in his brain and as he moved away from her, his index fingers moved up and down, in a wave that resembled *The Wiggles* signature move. He turned away with horror.

What was that?

He had never waved like that in his life. His hands seemed to have been possessed by some evil being determined to ruin his life. He sped up. Two older boys raced past him, slamming into his shoulder as they passed. The bus line was reverberating with excited energy. He couldn't face it today, so he started the long walk home, even though it would take him over an hour. Ethan's face coloured with each step, reliving all the painful details of their conversation.

What now? Was that it? Would they just fizzle out? Perhaps they'd never existed. His almost, not quite, barely-there girlfriend. But there *was* something. Or had been. The drawings they exchanged in art. The way they found each other side by side in the canteen line. Shared sniggering every time Mr Allan said the word 'unacceptable'. But that was all before this. The universe was clearly against him ever having a girlfriend.

He kicked a rock along the deserted dirt road, as the faint sound of a tractor's engine buzzed in his ears. Why did he have to leave her with that as a final memory? The principal said they could be doing home schooling for six months and all Ethan could do was wave his fingers at her like a children's entertainer?

He dumped his bag at the front door, hungry and sweaty. His mum was leaning against the fridge and staring into a small wooden box. The kitchen table was covered in papers and junk from the garage. Mum loved a good clean-out. She stood straight and re-arranged her face when he walked in.

'Hi.' She placed the box on the table. 'I heard they're closing the schools.'

'Yep.'

'We're not even really supposed to go out,' Mum said, watching him.

'Yeah, heard that.' Ethan reached for the peanut butter and slapped two bits of bread on the bench.

'What about Mila?'

The name hit him in the gut. Ethan instantly regretted mentioning her. It was a moment of weakness on his part. A naive optimism that he would soon be bringing her home for dinner and hanging out in his bedroom listening to music. Mum had tried to play it cool at the time, but since then, she'd been bringing it up at every opportunity.

'What about her?' he replied.

'Well, did you make plans to stay in touch?'

'We're not together or anything Mum. We don't have to stay in touch.' He slathered the peanut butter on the bread and slapped it together in punishment.

Mum raised her eyebrows at him. He waited for her to say something about him not using a breadboard, but she said nothing. Her desire to talk about Mila clearly outweighed cleanliness in this situation.

'Anyway, she doesn't have a phone,' he continued.

'Oh. Okay. Yeah, they must struggle with all those children. Have they got power and everything back yet?'

He shrugged and shoved the peanut butter sandwich in his mouth.

'Well, you'll have to woo her the old-fashioned way.' She ruffled his hair. 'Through letters or something.'

The dread in his stomach returned as the peanut butter moved slowly down his throat. If he needed to woo her through letters or words or anything to do with the English language, then he was doomed.

***

Hazel lifted the lid of the letterbox and her insides clenched. Nothing. She dropped the lid and it made a mocking hollow bang. She turned and walked back up the path to the house, trying not catch her mother's eye.

***

Ethan stopped drawing the fly. His notepad was full of drawings of insects. Pictures seemed so much easier than words. He sat down in front of his laptop. Mum was doing her last shift at the RSL today, so this was probably the last chance to have the house to himself. It was even quieter than normal. He could even hear the cows from Mrs Bunch's property two kilometres away. He breathed in and checked Mila's school email address again. Tap. Tap. Tap. He concentrated hard on putting the letters down one after the other. A voice he hadn't heard in years replayed in his head. *Hey Ethan, how do you spell cat? What about dog?* Followed by kids' laughter. He bit his lip and squinted hard at the screen. Tap. Tap. Tap. The words moved in front of him. The red lines highlighting his spelling mistakes jumped out at him. Thirty minutes passed but finally he had something.

Hey, how's it going? Been anywhere good lately. Nope me neither ha-ha. He read it back to himself.

Lame. So lame.

Ethan held his finger down on the delete key until the hard-won letters disappeared.

It needed to be funnier. Smarter. Better.

***

Another day. Another empty letterbox.

***

Ethan jumped out of bed and reached for his laptop. Something had come to him in the night. He tapped slowly.

Hey, miss ya! What's happening?

He sat back in his bed and rubbed his hands through his hair. Nup, that's not right either. It had only been two weeks, he couldn't say that he missed her yet. Even though he did. Seeing her at school each day had given his life a brightness that he couldn't explain. The tiny moments, like his shoulder touching hers as they walked to class together. Her laugh when he'd drawn a picture of Mr Allan on her maths book. Was it all in his head? Maybe. But without her, he felt he was merely existing, not living. And now she was over thirty kilometres away on her farm with her parents and a thousand siblings. Ethan and Mila (if there even was such a thing) was fading into nothingness.

***

The scarf was as long as her leg now, but Hazel kept going. The repetition gave her comfort and purpose. Her nightdress flapped in the cool night air as she sat on the veranda and looked up at the moon. She thought back to his words in the very first letter: *The days are hard. The nights even harder. But knowing we are under the same moon gives me hope.*

***

Ethan sat down at the laptop again. He would send something tonight, even if it was the worst thing that one human has ever sent to another human.

The blank screen and blinking cursor mocked him.

And no words came. Not a single one.

He shut his laptop with a bang.

It would be weird to email now anyway. He grabbed his pencil and continued his drawing of the fly trapped in an intricate spider's web. At first, the fly had been his focus. A bulging eyed-creature with delicate wings. But each day he had added a further grey rung to the web so that the fly appeared smaller and smaller and the web bigger and bigger. Then he grabbed a tennis ball and started hitting it against the wall. The beat was loud and satisfying. Fortunately, Mum was still in the garage cleaning out stuff from a thousand years ago. He walked to the kitchen to find something sweet.

The dining table was still covered in junk. The weird brown box was resting on the kitchen counter. Since Mum wasn't getting any more shifts, her 're-organising' had gone up a level. Mum had threatened to start on his wardrobe next.

He picked up the box and examined it. Maybe it was filled with valuable old coins? He'd seen *Antiques Roadshow* with Mum, some of that stuff was worth heaps.

The box groaned slightly as he opened it. His nose twitched from the dust. No coins, just a bunch of old papers. He picked up one of the bits of paper. The words and letters squiggled in front of him, almost like they were moving on the page. It was even harder to read than typed letters. He could only make out a few words. *Dear … miss … love*.

Ethan shut the box and went back to staring at the near empty fridge.

***

Hazel wrapped the scarf around and around her neck and face until all that was poking out was her eyes. She laughed at herself in the mirror and then sat back on her bed. Her mother was right. It was a ridiculous length, and she should probably start something new. But to stop felt like giving up on this one and she wasn't quite ready to do that.

***

He threw the drawing on the bed and walked to the kitchen. The spider's web was so big you would be forgiven for missing the fly completely. As he gulped down a banana, Ethan noticed the brown box was still on the kitchen bench. He picked it up and stared at the papers again. They looked like letters. Like, really, really old letters. He squinted hard to work out what they said. Figures jumped and moved around like a jigsaw puzzle, like they always did. But the running writing made it even harder than normal. He tried again.

I've missed you.

He stopped chewing and read on.

Knowing we are under the same moon gives me hope.

He stared hard at the next set of words.

It feels as if I've been away so long, I've almost forgotten the smell of your hair and the softness of your hand in mine. Almost.

Whoa.

Instinctively, he dropped the paper to the ground. Like stumbling across an intimate moment between two lovers. But he was frozen in the spot and couldn't walk away. Those words. Whoever wrote them obviously didn't have a problem with them, like him.

Ethan picked up the letter and stared at the name of the top. *To H.* It was signed, *Yours truly, G.* Well, G was one smooth operator, whoever he was.

He placed the letters neatly back in the box and took it into his room. Without thinking, he sat on his bed and reached for his laptop again. His fingers moved quickly.

Hey. How's it going? Haven't seen you in ages. Almost forgotten the sound of your laugh. Almost.

He paused and his finger hovered over the 'send' button. It came down with a light click.

***

She wouldn't check the letterbox at all today. No, she wouldn't.

***

Three days later and no reply. He'd checked his inbox literally 47 times the day before. Nothing. Nada. Zip.

Each time he logged on was like a kick to the guts.

The pain was worse than the unending boredom and loneliness that had preceded it.

He'd been an idiot to put himself out there so completely. Mila would probably show it to her friends and laugh at the mistakes he'd undoubtedly made.

***

Was he alive? Injured maybe? The dark thoughts came with the dark light. She didn't even flinch when she heard the postman now.

At 3:03pm on Thursday, Ethan checked his inbox for the 32nd time when it pinged into sight.

From: Mila Ristevski

Lol thanks. All good here. We've got a laptop from the school now and the internet is working! The boys driving me round the bend ☹ *I miss your drawings.*

He inhaled and then a broad smile crossed his face. He read it again. She missed his drawings.

The letters arrived at once. All four of them with different dates. As though they had met up somewhere along the postal line and decided to stick together. An ocean of words that were tender and familiar and loving. Hazel spun around and reached for the green yarn to start something new.

His Mum popped her head into his room. 'Hey mate, have you seen an old brown box anywhere?'

His head jerked up. 'Um.'

'It had a bunch of old papers in it. Belonged to my grandmother.'

'Grandmother?'

'Yeah, I've been meaning to show you actually. It has some cool letters from my Pop to her.'

The box sat on his desk as Ethan finished the latest email to Mila. His Mum was delighted that he wanted to keep it in his room. Things seemed heaps easier now. He'd read all of Great Pop's letters, but nothing seemed to work as well as his own words. He still made mistakes but spellcheck picked up the e's that should have been o's and he wasn't so stressed about it anyway. He'd even told Mila about taking inspiration from his Great Pop and Mila had actually replied:

That is hilarious. Not that it ever mattered what you wrote or the way you wrote it. I just like you.

She just likes him.

Ethan read his email once more and pressed the send button.

The Dark Day

Peter Clarkson

I'd never really paid much attention to the sun. It'd always just been up there, day after day, pumping out heat and light. Like clockwork.

The sun's light travels at—you guessed it—the speed of light. But how fast is that? 299,792,458 metres per second. It's like some kind of cosmic speed limit. Nothing in the universe can travel faster than that. Who set it at that speed? Maybe it was God. Maybe it was random chance or some consequence of the Big Bang. It doesn't much matter.

What I can't wrap my head around is that even though light travels at such a fantastic speed, it still takes the sun's light a whole eight minutes and twenty seconds to reach us here on Earth.

What's more incredible, is that on the Dark Day, it took even longer.

***

Emily and I had finished our exams, so we'd driven up the coast to spend the holidays together. Looking back, I think we were just doing anything we could to dodge our parents.

We sat on the beach and listened to the white noise of the ocean. Emily's long, slender legs stretched out across the sand next to mine. Her face was concealed by a hat and sunglasses, both absurdly oversized. It made her look glamorous and me feel inadequate, as I sat there in my baggy shorts and T-shirt which concealed a body that, to be honest, could have belonged to a thirteen-year-old boy.

The sun looked like a warm egg yolk slipping down the surface of the sky and into the water. I glanced at it, then closed my eyes to watch the electric flickers of yellow and red dance across my eyelids.

'Jocelyn and I need your help,' Emily said, holding out her arms.

I rose to help her up. 'Don't start naming it, Em.'

'*It?*' She took off her sunglasses and that single dimple appeared on her left cheek as she smiled in mock offence. '*Her.*'

'Probably just a blob.'

'Jocelyn's a beautiful name. And it *is* a girl.'

How women claim to know these things remains a mystery to me, but there was something behind her eyes in that moment which made me believe her.

We held hands as we ambled barefoot through the sand and along the narrow path which cut through the beach grass and back up to the road. It was that time of the afternoon in early summer when the heat of the day lingered, but the chill of the coming night could be felt too.

There was a clearing at the top of the beach, ringed by weeping peppermints, where we'd parked the caravan. I shivered as the wind swept across the small picnic area there. It lifted the loose, sandy soil and formed miniature dust tornadoes that wreaked their havoc for a brief moment before falling back to the earth.

We'd set up our fold-out bed under the canvas awning. Walls of thick, clear plastic extended down from it, creating an outdoor room. It provided some relief from the heat of the day and a chance to sleep among the stars on a summer night.

***

The wind was tapping the awning, as if it were asking to be let inside.

I reached over to Emily's side of the bed and found it empty.

There were footsteps inside the caravan and then came the sound of liquid gurgling into the drain underneath. There were more thumps and thuds, until finally the door clicked open and orange light spilled out.

'Oz,' Emily said. Her loud voice made me flinch. 'You awake?'

'Yeah.'

'What time is it?'

I lifted an arm out from under the blanket, reached down to the sandy floor and padded around for my clothes. I gathered the material into a ball and squeezed until I found the hard rectangle inside. 'Ten past eight. You makin' coffee?'

'You sure?'

'Reckon I'll need two,' I said as I lay back down.

'Check your phone again.'

I groaned as I brought the phone up to my face. 'Still 8:10, Em. Check back with me in ten seconds and it'll be 8:11.'

She turned and stepped back inside the caravan, leaving the door open.

I fumbled in the darkness for my clothes and struggled to put them on.

Pressing down on my phone, I lit a path to the corner of the awning, unzipped the plastic sheets and stepped out into the night. The world was shrouded in a heavy blanket of darkness. I could barely see the silhouette of the treeline against the sky.

Somewhere, down the hill, the ocean rolled on.

Emily stumbled down the steps of the caravan behind me. I reached back through the plastic and held up my phone to light her way over.

'It's ten past eight alright,' I said as she joined me in the gloom.

'Where the hell's the morning?'

'Weird, isn't it?' She stared up at the sky, spread her arms and turned in a circle.

I cleared my throat. 'An eclipse, maybe?'

'Maybe,' Emily said. 'But there's no stars.'

I kept pressing down on my phone to keep some light between us. 'No reception,' I said. 'You?'

'Can't find my phone.'

'And what's that smell?'

Emily paused to take a deep breath. 'Dunno.'

'What do we do?'

Emily stepped over to me, turned and rested her back against my chest. She took my hands and wrapped my arms around her. 'Let's have breakfast and give it some time,' she said. 'If there's no change, we'll drive down to Madden and see if we can find out what's going on.'

'Okay.'

Emily traced her fingers up and down my arm as we stood there, staring out into the abyss.

***

'Let's leave this thing here,' I said as I unhitched the caravan from the car. The red glow of the car's taillights provided just enough light to perform the operation. 'No point towing it down to Madden and back. I can barely reverse it in the daylight.' I was trying to sound casual, but I felt short of breath as I spoke. 'D'you think it's dark everywhere?'

'I'm sure it's just temporary,' Emily said as she got into the car.

I joined her and put the car in gear. 'Sounds crazy, but maybe the Earth's stopped spinning. Or maybe it's slowed down and the people on the other side are sitting around wondering when night'll finally come?'

'I doubt it.'

I could tell Emily wasn't in the mood for speculating, but I couldn't stop. 'Could the sun have just burned out?'

'That'd be more of a gradual thing, yeah? It was so hot yesterday. Surely the sun can't just go out like a candle.' She reached over and placed her hand on my knee. 'It's going to be alright, Oz.'

Our headlights carved a path through the darkness as we pulled out of the clearing and onto the serpentine road. The world beyond the car was nebulous. I imagined the ocean to our right and the hills to our left as we edged along. I kept reminding myself that a new day had begun—that it was almost ten o'clock.

It struck me that we might not find anyone in Madden. After all, we hadn't seen any other cars on the road. Perhaps there'd been some awful cataclysm and we'd somehow been spared.

Emily shot upright in her chair. 'The radio!'

How silly it was to not have thought of that.

She flicked through the preset stations, but there was only static.

***

Streetlights appeared on the sides of the road as we entered Madden and, along with the lights glowing inside people's homes, the eerie darkness was easier to ignore. Other cars appeared on the road and we slowed as we entered the main street. It was a relief to see so many others.

I parked and checked my phone as I shut off the engine. 'Still nothing.'

'Me neither,' Emily said. 'How 'bout we find a shop and get some food and things? Then we can walk around and see what we can find out.'

It felt good to be heading off with a purpose.

We found a strip of shops, all closed, except for a petrol station and adjoining store. Emily went in and I remained outside, under a blinking streetlight. Three men were sitting at a small table by the entrance to the store. One of them was pointing to the sky and speaking in earnest to his companions about an alien invasion. 'War o' the Worlds, mate - that's what this is. Invade under the cover of darkness.' The suggestion made my shoulders bounce in silent laughter as I turned away. Though, I must admit, the suggestion lingered in my mind a little longer than I thought it might.

***

The flow of people was toward the other end of the street, in the direction of where I thought the beach must be. A crowd was gathering at what we found was a small church there. It was a modern, pale-bricked building and the only indication of its identity was a sign which faced the road. I managed a smile as I read the black letters on the glowing white background: *'I'm also making a list and checking it twice' - God.*

We edged our way through the foyer and into the main room. Though I've only been inside a church a handful of times, there was that somehow familiar, musty smell. Thick wooden beams spanned the ceiling, rising at a gentle angle from the back to a platform at the front. The bench seating was filled, although some people were kneeling. New arrivals were huddling at the edges of the room and at the ends of the rows. Some children sat cross-legged in the space in front of the platform.

A plainly dressed woman, the priest, probably in her forties, was pacing slowly as she addressed the group. Her long hair was frizzy and touched with grey. 'It's a belief so firm that that we consider it unshakeable fact. The sun's risen every other morning. And yet,' she paused, 'it hasn't risen today.' She checked her watch. 'And it's close to midday now.'

People continued to shuffle in, filling the empty spaces. The priest smiled at them and continued. 'But we know it's not entirely correct to speak of the sun rising, because it's us here on Earth that revolve around it. Spinning.' She held up a finger and traced an invisible circle in the air. 'Causing the sun to move across our sky.

'Has something large passed between us and the sun? I don't know. Has our sun faltered momentarily? I don't know. Has God seen fit to take our light away? I don't know. I don't think so. The sun hasn't risen and there's a reason for it. Whatever it is, it's out of our control. It'll become clear soon enough.'

She paused to let her words settle over her audience. 'Whatever the explanation is for what's happening, God knows it. The sun is the largest object in our solar system, but it's worth reminding ourselves that it's not the most powerful. Don't be overcome by fear. Gather. Be with your families. Help others where you can.

'We'll be sharing some food in a little while and you're all welcome to stay. We'll pass on any new information as it comes in.'

Towards the front of the room a thin man in a cap raised his hand and the priest motioned for him to speak. 'What if it's gone for good?' He stood up, turned and regarded the crowd. 'What then?'

The priest offered him the palms of her hands. 'It won't do us any good to think like that.'

The murmuring of the crowd grew louder. Emily lifted her eyebrows and nodded towards the exit.

'She's right,' she said, as we spilled out into the street. 'There must be some cause for all this.'

'That guy in the church had a point though. How long would we last?'

Emily didn't answer.

'D'you believe in God?'

My question hovered in the air as we walked back to the car.

***

We'd driven back to the caravan and then further up the coast, searching for phone reception, without luck. Eventually, we found ourselves back in the main street of Madden.

Even though we were exhausted, neither of us had been able to sleep. I had a terrible headache. Although we didn't say it out loud,

102

we knew we were both holding out for the sunrise.

Cars lined both sides of the road and several had their headlights on. Through the foggy windscreen we watched as more and more people gathered on a football oval beside the church. Small fires and portable lights illuminated the area.

I turned on the radio and let the static buzz at low volume. 'Heard this one before,' Emily said. She was sipping Coke through a straw.

'Maybe you should cut out the junk,' I said. 'I don't know, get some of those special vitamins and all that?'

'Don't be stupid, Oz .'

'Should we get married?' The words were out of my mouth before I could catch them.

Emily went into a coughing fit. I think some Coke came out of her nose. 'See previous answer.'

When she recovered, she set the can down on the dashboard and burped. 'Let's take it one step at a time. Only fools rush in and all that.'

'We were careful,' I said. 'How'd it happen?'

'Well Daddy-o, a wise man once told me that there aren't any mistakes in life. Just happy accidents.'

'Who said that? Wait—don't tell me.' Those words were rattling around somewhere in the messy filing cabinet of my mind.

'Give up?'

'Okay.'

'Bob Ross.'

We burst out laughing. 'A wise man indeed,' I said. 'I'd love to see a happy little cloud right about now.'

'Me too.'

'So,' I said, keeping my eyes on the windscreen, 'will your Dad freak?'

Emily picked up the can and drained it. 'Prob'ly.'

'But we are, you know,' I searched for the right word, 'of age.'

'Maybe this whole eternal darkness thing will be a good distraction?' Emily said. 'He can't shoot you if he can't see you.'

I managed a laugh. 'Not sure which scares me more.'

'Yeah.'

I leaned forward and looked up at the sky. 'I'm going out of my mind trying to figure it out. If the sun's up there and the world's spinning, how come there was no day?'

'Dunno.' Emily unclipped her seatbelt. 'Reckon we should head out there and see what's happening?' She opened her door and stepped out before I could answer.

Emily hobbled across the road and onto the grass ahead of me, as if she was walking on hot coals.

'Why don't you just put your thongs on?' I said.

'I'll be right,' she said, standing a little straighter.

The priest we'd heard speak the day before smiled as we ducked under the metal rail which ran around the boundary of the oval. 'Keeping warm?'

'Not really,' Emily said. 'I'm Emily. This is Osmo.'

The priest grinned. '*Osmo?*'

'I get that a lot,' I said.

'No, I like it,' she said. She reached out and touched my arm as she spoke. 'My name's Cathie. We've got quite a party here now. People's spirits are up now that dawn's getting close. Have you two eaten?'

I nodded. 'D'you really expect it to come back?'

'You bet,' she said. 'I expect the sun to rise every morning. For it not to yesterday was a surprise. For it to not rise again would be something else.' I saw that hope was this woman's currency and she had enough to dispense to anyone who needed it. Still, it was nice to know that someone believed so firmly that the sun would return.

Emily was nodding as Cathie spoke. 'What time's it due?'

'5:25,' replied Cathie. She bent down and held her watch close to her eyes. 'So, we're at T-minus eight minutes. East is that way,' she pointed back over our heads, inland, anticipating Emily's next question. 'The sunrise here is absolutely gorgeous.'

I realised that everyone was facing us, staring in the direction Cathie had pointed. Some people were sitting on camping chairs, others were huddled on the ground underneath blankets.

As the minutes passed the crowd grew quieter.

We waited, listening to the sound of the waves crashing on the beach behind us.

I'd spent so many hours waiting for this moment, I wasn't sure how I'd react. If there were some sudden danger, I knew that I could do no more than simply surrender to it. I felt like a child forced to endure some awful carnival ride, gripping the handrail and praying that the ordeal would soon come to an end.

There was a delirium of the body, as well as the mind. To upset the natural rhythm of day and night was to unsettle that animal part of us. That inner clock with which our minds and bodies normally kept time. I felt the springs and pulleys inside my mind slackening as the minutes ticked by.

A bird whistled and then fell silent again.

I wasn't sure if anyone else heard it.

Faint embers started to glow above the treeline.

I felt the muscles in my shoulders relax.

I stood unmoved. Eyes locked on the horizon.

Waiting for the uppermost edge of the sun to appear.

I stumbled as Emily wrapped her arms around me and I became aware of the cheering all around. She whispered in my ear, 'Can we go home now?'

We held each other as the rising sun bathed the world in more and more light.

But it was a strange kind of muted light, as if the sun was

burning at half strength.

The sky was a murky purple and smudged with grimy clouds.

The trees that surrounded the field faded into view. They looked weary and grey, as if they hadn't slept either. Their limbs drooped, like they were carrying invisible suitcases.

***

We drove back up the coast to collect the caravan with the windows all the way down. I held an open hand against the rushing wind.

A band of sky above the horizon, out to sea, was blue and clear, but above that was ever-darkening shades of purple.

The sun was an orange disc glowing behind a hazy curtain.

Short bursts of music started to break through the static on the radio and then Emily's phone pinged.

I gave her a moment to flick through the messages.

'Aah,' she said, bent over the phone. 'That makes sense.'

'What does?'

She gave me a sideways glance and nodded. 'I knew it would be something like that.'

There was that dimple again.

'Like what?' I closed my window. 'What is it?'

'Hang on a sec,' she said and lay back in her chair. She put her feet up on the dashboard and tapped away on the screen.

'You know,' I said, 'it's not safe to sit like that. What are you writing?'

'A message.'

'To who?'

'Mum and Dad. Just telling them we're okay,' she looked up from the phone, 'and that we have some good news.'

'Em, don't.'

'Too late!' she said, then tossed the phone into the back of the car. 'He'll probably be happy for us. Mum will be.'

I saw that Emily's hands were resting on her belly.

I reached over and put a hand on hers. 'So, what does Jocelyn think about all this?'

Emily smiled. 'She's excited.'

'Me too,' I said.

'Me three.'

'Well,' I said. 'Are you going to tell me?'

'About what?'

'Whatever it is,' I mocked her high-pitched voice, 'that makes *so much sense.*'

Emily retrieved her phone from the back seat. She sat up straight and cleared her throat. 'The sun returned to the skies of south-western Australia this morning, bringing an end to thirty-two hours of near-total darkness. Thermal satellite images show that a volcano on Heard Island, an isolated and uninhabited island in the Southern Ocean, erupted two days ago. The massive explosion propelled trillions of cubic metres of ash and gas into the atmosphere, which then drifted four thousand kilometers to enshroud much of the West Australian coast. The energy released from the explosion is estimated to be equal to around three hundred megatons of TNT.'

I pulled the car over, onto the gravel by the side of the road. 'Now, I'm no expert,' Emily said, 'but that sounds like a lot of TNT.'

I leaned over and pinched her leg. 'What do you mean you knew it would be something like that?'

She squealed and swatted my hand away. 'Well, I didn't think the world was ending!'

I grinned and nodded. 'Neither did I.'

'Yeah, right.'

Emily's phone sprang to life and we both jumped.

Our eyes met as the tinny, electronic melody played on.

'Okay,' I said as I turned off the engine. 'Put it on speaker.'

Silencing the Storm

Geraldine Borella

Jolie pulls up short in a tunnel lined with rings of gold; clouds of blue, green, and grey swirl about her. *What is this place?* A second ago, she'd been running through the pine forest, racing to get away from Cleo and Ed.

She listens. Aside from the dull yet insistent thump of blood through her veins, and the in and out of her rapid breathing, there's no sound: no bird calls, no rustle of wind, no snap of sticks or scrunch of dried pine needles underfoot, and thankfully, no more calls from Cleo.

'How could they?' cries Jolie.

She turns to face from where she came and closes her eyes, but the image of her best friend kissing her boyfriend down by the lake won't clear.

'Jolie! Wait up!' Cleo had yelled.

She'd chased after Jolie, yelling explanations for why stealing the one good thing in Jolie's life was necessary, unavoidable even. *Well, screw her and her need to be in the spotlight twenty-four seven.*

Jolie turns back around and steps further into the tunnel. It's like standing in the middle of an ominous, yet silent storm. Strangely though, she feels at peace. Her breathing slows and the pounding of her heart dulls. As she takes another step forward, approaching the next golden ring, she marvels at the clouds that merge and morph into different shapes and colours.

Am I dead? Is this some sort of afterlife? So dreamy and floaty, nothing penetrates this space, she can leave everything behind. Cleo and Ed, school, and most of all, the warzone of home, her mother and father fighting about money non-stop.

Another step forward. Where will this tunnel lead? To a better life? To her death? She can't say, but she can't stay in this void forever, no matter how comforting or peaceful it is. She stops and shakes her head. She's never won a thing in all of her fifteen years. Why would luck be on her side now? So, she turns and walks back towards the entrance. It's a crappy life, but at least it's her crappy life.

The view is the same in all directions, a swirling, dark, but colourful storm, the pine forest nowhere to be seen. Her heart rate quickens. What if she can't return? What if she's stuck here forever? *Just walk, Jolie,* she tells herself, and within a few steps she's back in the forest, back with the birds and the whispering wind. She looks around for Cleo but there's no sign of her. Maybe she's given up and gone home? At least Jolie hopes so.

She turns to check for the tunnel entrance but it's not there anymore. All she sees is more pine forest, but it's not quite the same as she left it. The trees are taller, their trunks wider and there's less undergrowth, dried pine needles carpeting the forest floor.

Jolie continues towards home, trying to shake off the strangeness.

But as she walks through town, things get weirder still. The Grapevine Café is gone, a McDonald's in its place, sprung up overnight. Jolie glances about, confused. The main street now has two lanes each way, cars and trucks flowing fast, and there are traffic lights too. *What the hell's going on?*

When she gets to Peppertree Close, the houses are different.

The Altman's fibro cottage is gone, and a huge concrete building looms in its place. It's a block of flats, the sort you might see in Brisbane. Other houses are painted different colours, some gone completely, vacant lots in their place. The merry-go-round in the park where Jolie escapes to each night—to spin, watch the stars, and smoke cigarettes stolen from Mum—is gone, the whole park now a set of shops. Did she turn the wrong way in that tunnel?

She wanders further down Peppertree Close, wondering if her house will be there, and breathes a sigh of relief to find it is. It's rundown, the paint peeling and curling off the timber siding, the iron roof patchworked with brown-orange rust and the front steps almost rotted away. But the mailbox still has that crudely painted sign on top, the one she and Dad had made: *Wyndham's—Stick Ya Junk Mail Somewhere Else!*

Jolie climbs the rotting stairs, taking care to tread lightly, then fishes her house key out of her backpack. But the key won't work the lock.

She knocks. 'Mum?' No answer, so she knocks again. Her mother should be home. She's always home after school. 'Mum?' she calls.

Just as she's about to go around the side of the house, to shimmy through her bedroom window, the door opens. An old woman with white curly hair answers and peers at Jolie, squinting hard.

'Jolie?' she gasps, before collapsing to the floor.

'Mum?' whispers Jolie.

***

An ambulance ferries them to hospital, the paramedic concerned Jolie's mother, Irene, may have sustained a brain bleed in the fall. She'd struck her head on the doorframe and had seemed confused when she'd come to.

'That's my daughter,' she keeps telling the paramedic. 'Come back from the dead after thirty-two years and not a day older. Look at her!'

The paramedic pats her hand and checks her pulse. 'Tell me your name again, love.'

'Irene Wyndham,' she says, a note of annoyance in her voice.

'And what day is it?' asks the paramedic.

Irene snorts. 'It's Wednesday July 3rd, 2019, but I'm trying to tell you something important—'

The paramedic smiles. 'Good, Irene, that's right, it is Wednesday.' The paramedic smiles sadly at Jolie as the ambulance sails through the traffic lights. 'Don't worry about your gran,' he whispers. 'She'll be in good hands at the hospital.'

Jolie nods, unsure what to say.

When the CT scan shows her mum really is okay, Jolie confirms Irene's bizarre story to the social worker, and the police are called in.

***

'I can't believe you rang the newspapers,' Jolie says as she peeks through the timber-look venetian blinds.

Her mother shrugs and scrolls on her iPad, no doubt searching for more porcelain figurines to add to her collection. The house is filled with them: ladies in period ballgowns, ballerinas mid-pose, Spanish dancers holding fans and castanets, German boys and girls in traditional dress, French can-can dancers in ruffled skirts. Jolie's bedroom has been completely taken over with the collection, all trace of Jolie gone.

'It's a different world nowadays, love,' says Irene. 'You gotta play the game.' Jolie watches over her mother's shoulder as Irene clicks on a picture of a porcelain milkmaid priced at $350. 'How do you think I got all this?' says Irene, gesturing at the renovated interior of the house. The tattered linoleum has been replaced by timber floorboards and the tacky fake wood wall-cladding is gone too. A huge flatscreen TV sits on the wall and the brown velvet lounge suite has been updated to black leather. The kitchen's had a makeover as well, grey tiles lining the floor, the lime green Laminex replaced by stone, stainless steel and wood. 'Now you're back,' says Irene, 'we're in the news again. Hot property. Might even get enough money to do the outside of the house this time.'

Jolie sighs and peeks through the blinds again. Peppertree Close has become host to a multitude. Crackpots line the streets, camping in vans and old buses, waving signs about alien invasion, while others hold vigil for the coming of Armageddon. Media vans with satellite dishes stake out the house, waiting to shove microphones into Jolie's face if she ever happens to step outdoors, which she doesn't. She hides away inside, trying to process it all, writing swear words over and over in the 'feelings journal' the hospital psychologist had given her.

'I'm in talks with several TV networks,' says Irene, as she puts down the iPad and lights a cigarette. 'Playing them off against each other.' She grins, as though proud of herself. 'See if we can't get them to sharpen their pencils.'

Jolie sneers. She doesn't want to 'play the game', be interviewed on TV, paraded as a freak, just so her mother can get a new roof on the house and more figurines for her collection. She *wants* her old life back.

'Are you ever going to tell me what happened to Dad?' she asks, as she turns away from the window. Irene draws on her cigarette and holds her breath. Her mother has been evasive, dismissive even, but Jolie needs answers. Exhaling smoke, Irene bends to flick ash into the crystal ashtray on the marble coffee table.

'He passed eleven years ago. What more do you need to know?'

Jolie's throat aches and her voice comes out wobbly and weak. The last time she saw her father they'd fought. She'd said horrible things, things she now can't take back. 'How?' she says, wiping the tears that spill onto her cheeks. '*How* did he die? What happened, Mum? I need you to tell me.' Doesn't she get it? It might be old news to her mother but to Jolie, it's like he's died a week ago.

Irene sniffs. 'He couldn't take it, that's all. Couldn't take not knowing what happened.' She shrugs, draws again on her cigarette. 'Killed himself, drink-driving. Stupid idiot.'

'Don't call him that,' snarls Jolie. 'Just … *don't*, okay! God, poor Dad.' Jolie slumps onto the lounge, lowers her head and sobs into her hands as her mother huffs and clicks her tongue.

'Poor Dad?' she snipes. 'How about poor me? He left me to do everything. Spent his time wallowing and drinking, while I had to work, deal with the police and the media, and keep on looking for you.' She jabs at her chest with her thumb. '*I'm* the one you should feel sorry for, not him.' Her mouth twists into a bitter grimace. 'I lost everything: my daughter, my husband, my life. And now look at me—I'm old and had it—and just when I should be relaxing, I'm stuck raising a teenager.'

She scowls, stubs her cigarette into the ashtray and stalks out of the room.

***

'It's probably the new guard clocking on,' says Irene when she gets up to answer the knock at the front door. The police, stationed at the front gate to keep the crowd at bay, check in every change of shift. But it's not them at all, it's a middle-aged woman. She barges past Irene and stomps through to the kitchen.

'I need to see her,' she yells. 'With me own eyes.'

'How'd you get past the guard, Cleo?' demands Irene.

Jolie glances up, a spoon filled with cereal and milk poised ready, and gapes at the woman with the skunk streak of grey hair carving its way through a badly home-dyed mahogany red. *Cleo?!* Dressed in a black velour tracksuit with large-framed sunnies perched on top of her head, the woman's nothing like Jolie's Cleo. Where was the slim, tanned, beautiful teenage girl who could get any boy she wants, even Ed?

'You're just the same,' yells Cleo. 'Look at you! I don't know how, but you're just the same. And got your whole life ahead of you.

Not like me.' She sniffs and then points a leopard-printed talon at Jolie. 'You ruined my life.'

Jolie drops her spoon. The last time she saw Cleo, she was attached by the lips to her boyfriend. But somehow Jolie has ruined *her* life?

'I what…?' splutters Jolie. Her heart rate rises, and she can hear the blood roaring through her veins. Her legs are jelly, her chest tight.

'You heard me. For all this time everyone thought I knew something, that I knew what happened to you.' She gestures wildly. 'But here you are! And famous.' She stares with open hatred. 'Some even pegged me as a murderer. Can you imagine? *Me*, a murderer! You *ruined* me, Jolie Wyndham, completely ruined me.'

'That's enough,' spits Irene. 'You need to leave, before I call the police in.'

Something snaps in Jolie. She's never stood up to Cleo before, has always backed down from a fight, stayed quiet, toed the line. But not now, not after what she's done. If Cleo hadn't kissed Ed down at the lake, then Jolie wouldn't have gone into that tunnel, her father would still be alive, and her mother wouldn't be so old and bitter. If anything, it's Cleo's fault, the lot of it.

'I really don't know how I could be to blame for all *that*.' Jolie gestures with a hand at Cleo, while visually mapping the lumps and bumps in her velour tracksuit pants. '*You* made your choices, not me.'

'You absolute hag!' Cleo moves towards Jolie, pushing a kitchen chair to the floor.

'Enough!' yells Irene. She grabs a frying pan from the sink drainer and raises it high. 'Get out! *Now!*

***

Jolie needs fresh air and a perm. Her curls have all but grown out and she's spent the last few days inside, stalking old school friends online. With the help of her mother, she created a fake profile, but instead of grounding her, it's left her feeling disconnected, out-of-place. Her school friends have got careers, houses, children—some even have grandchildren—and *she's* still a fifteen-year-old girl. She needs to get out and about, see a friendly face, and she knows where to find one.

'I'm going to Lynelle's,' she says at breakfast.

'Lynelle died over fifteen years ago, love,' Irene tells her. 'Breast cancer. Her salon's still there, but with new owners.'

Jolie's breath catches in her throat. 'I'll go somewhere else then.' Everything's changed, everything's wrong. Retracing her steps and sitting in Lynelle's old salon without Lynelle will only make her feel worse.

'Your call,' shrugs Irene. 'But don't get anything special. It's not as if I can afford it right now. At least not until you agree to that interview.'

Ignoring that last barb, Jolie sneaks over the back fence and finds a budget hair salon in Main St, one that takes walk-ins. A middle-aged woman with thick strips of pink and purple in her blonde fringe greets her.

'Holy crap, it's you,' she squeals, clapping her hands together.

'Huh?'

'You haven't changed a bit. Not like me.' The woman giggles and the bubbly noise, followed by a snort, gives her away.

'Tracey-Anne Jensen?' whispers Jolie.

'In person,' winks the hairdresser. 'Though it's Tracey-Anne Sparrow now.'

Jolie gapes. 'You married Terry Sparrow?'

'No, silly,' giggles Tracey-Anne, rounding it off with another snort. 'I married Gerard, Terry's older brother.'

'Wow!' murmurs Jolie. 'Gerard drives that cool V8 ute. He's hot!'

Tracey-Anne cracks up laughing. 'Yeah, well, he still has a ute, but you might not think he's so hot now. He's bald and has a bit of a beer gut.' She nudges Jolie. 'Still gets me going though. If you know what I mean.' She winks and Jolie winces, feeling uncomfortable. It's like when her mother gave her that sex talk.

'So,' says Tracey-Anne. 'What are we going to do with this.' She gestures at Jolie's hair. 'We don't do perms now, so you'll have to choose some other style. Straight cuts are in. I reckon it'd suit your face shape.'

She guides Jolie to a chair, swishes a cape around her and clips it at the back. Spraying water, Tracey-Anne says, 'You were a right cow at school.'

'Huh?' says Jolie, suddenly aware of the scissors in Tracey-Anne's hands.

'Well … I guess Cleo was the main instigator, but you were just as bad, standing by and letting it all happen, egging it on even.' Tracey-Anne sets her spray bottle down and snips away at Jolie's locks. 'I often tell my girls about you two. Like, remember when Cleo read out my diary to the whole class? After Miss Jepson had to leave the room. Told all my secrets and laughed at every single one of them. That was the worst day of my life.'

Jolie shifts in her seat. 'I … ah …'

Tracey-Anne's hands are on her shoulders and she gives a gentle squeeze. 'Oh, don't stress,' she says, cutting hair again. 'It's all water under the bridge now.' She winks at Jolie's reflection but then her breezy smile disappears, and her stare turns icy. It's unsettling, and Jolie wants to tell her she'll go to another hairdresser, but the words won't come.

'You both called me Miss Piggy, remember?' says Tracey-Anne. She grabs a huge chunk of Jolie's fringe. 'I was stuck with that name all through school.' She cuts the chunk of hair in her hand and it falls into Jolie's lap. Jolie gapes at her reflection in the mirror. Her

116

fringe is high, jagged and crooked. Matched with the straight hair, it looks as though a bowl has been placed upside down on her head as a guide to cut around, while a toddler has gone crazy on her fringe.

Tracey-Anne sneers. 'That's for making my life miserable.' Then, she whips the cape away. 'This one's on me,' she says, quite cheerily. *'You're welcome!'*

***

Jolie hides for a week, still stinging. The haircut she can deal with, but Tracey-Anne's words ...? She'd never thought that deeply about her friendship with Cleo. Had she egged her on? Made her behaviour worse? Maybe. But for the most part she'd been relieved not to be on the receiving end. Maybe she *should* have stood up to her, stopped her being such a cow, but she'd had enough to deal with at home without creating more drama in her life.

'Jolie, for goodness sake,' snaps Irene, standing at the open refrigerator door. 'You've used all the milk again!' Her mother's sharp tone rips through her and the slam of the refrigerator door makes her jump. Will she ever feel calm again?

Jolie takes a deep breath. 'I barely had enough to cover my cereal. What do you want me to do? Have it with water?'

'Don't be smart, young lady. Money doesn't grow on trees, you know.'

Jolie mumbles, 'Why don't you sell a few figurines then, or better still, stop smoking.'

'I beg your pardon?' yells Irene.

Sitting up straight, Jolie preps for a fight. 'I said, why don't you—'

'I heard what you said, and you can take it back!' Irene glares, hands on hips. 'I've done everything for you, and yet you begrudge me a bit of enjoyment in my old age. You're so ungrateful. And I've only ever asked for *one* thing. Do that interview, and—'

'I'm not going on TV to be treated like a freak!' shouts Jolie.

They've had this out before, but it won't go away, Irene forever pushing.

'You expect me to keep paying your way then, do you?'

'Isn't that what parents *do*?'

Irene flushes red and spittle flies as she rants, 'You deprived me of all that, deprived me of being a mother. And now I'm expected to step up, when I *should* be enjoying grandchildren, not dealing with an ungrateful, selfish teenager who refuses to help.'

Jolie reels. 'How do you think I feel? Dad's dead. I have no friends. The world's completely different. I don't even have my clothes or my old bedroom anymore. It's clear you don't want me here, so maybe I should just leave.'

'It's always about you, isn't it?' says Irene as she lights another cigarette.

'Unbelievable.' Jolie drops her bowl into the sink and trudges to the small spare room where she's been sleeping. She packs a backpack with the 'feelings journal' and some of the awful op-shop clothes her mother bought, grabs some fruit and a packet of biscuits from the kitchen, and heads for the back door.

'Where are you going?' snaps Irene.

'Somewhere, *anywhere*. I'll catch a bus, get out of here.'

'Don't be such a drama queen,' scoffs Irene.

Jolie stares at her for a long moment, then shakes her head. 'Have a nice life,' she mumbles, then she leaves, slamming the back door. Rage spurs her on, over the neighbour's fence and through their yard. It drives her towards town, towards the bus station and beyond, and before long, without any conscious thought or decision, she's back in the pine forest near the lake. Back where it all began.

It's here she finds the translucent shimmering sphere, calling from deep within the pines. Wind wisps through the needled branches and she hears a soft hum as she approaches. The tunnel entices her forward, but she hesitates, biting her bottom lip. A part of her wants to run towards it before it disappears; another part wants to run away. Might it be better this time around, or worse? Would she go back in time, or move forward again? Would she get the opportunity to right wrongs? Be given a chance to live a newer, better life, knowing all that she knows now? She can't be sure. She can't be sure of anything anymore. Though there's one solid truth that seeps into her soul: the cocooning silence of the tunnel is far more peaceful than the storm raging in her head.

She thinks for a bit, then reaches into her backpack. If the sphere is still here when she's finished, she'll know what to do. With blank pages ripped from her journal, she grabs her pen and writes letters: to her mother, to Cleo, to Ed, to Tracey-Anne and to her form class. The sphere patiently shimmers and waits as she runs home, letters in hand.

She leaves her mother's on the back steps, placing a rock on top of it. The pages are packed with feelings, just as the psychologist suggested, telling her mother she loves her, that she misses the mum she remembers, the one uncorrupted by fame and money. She tells her she's sorry, but she has to move on, and she asks for forgiveness.

Then, she visits the cemetery. She kneels by her father's grave, running a finger over the brass lettering of his burial plaque, and talks. She talks for ages, then wipes her tears and says goodbye.

In town, she buys a large envelope and slips the remaining letters inside, addressing it to Tracey-Anne at Sassy Snips. *I could have done better*, she explains, *should have done better*, and suggests to Cleo and Ed that they could have too. Will Tracey-Anne read their letters before sending them on? It's possible; possible too that her words won't matter. But she can't change how others will remember her, or how they might choose to behave in the future; in the end she can only change herself, and she resolves to do so from this moment forward.

Back in the pine forest, the entrance to the tunnel shimmers and waits, as Jolie wavers. *Is running again really the answer?*

It waits as she paces about and mumbles. *But aren't I running towards life this time, not away from it?*

It waits as she rocks on her heels. *Only, what if things get worse? What if things get much worse?*

And it waits for one last moment as she takes a breath, wanting nothing more than to silence the raging storm within, and steps on through.

Escape

Elizabeth Macintosh

'What do you think you're doing?' Dad growls as he stands at the bedroom door.

My body shakes as I push clothes back into the wardrobe. *Keep your head down. Act calm.*

I hesitate, unsure of what to say. 'Oh, looking for a clean shirt.' I turn towards him, a blank look on my face. *Don't give anything away.* He stares, unsure of the validity of my answer.

'Well, hurry up, Kate! You need to feed those horses. Do it now or you'll get it!'

I will get it too. I wear the patchwork of green and purple bruises to prove it.

'Yes, Dad,' I reply hastily. *Don't make him angry. Agree.*

'And then you can cook dinner.' He holds my gaze.

'I'll just get some clean clothes first.' My heart thumps in the cage of my chest and my hands tremble as I make a show of finding a black long sleeved shirt. A favourite. The one that covers up the damage Dad inflicts. But he won't be doing that for much longer.

My father scratches his receding hairline, turns and walks away, his heavy frame just fitting through the doorway. I remove my barely soiled top and grimace as it pulls against a dark patch on my shoulder. Buttoning the clean shirt, I look in the mirror, pale blue eyes staring back, red curls pulled into a ponytail, a faded yellow mark on my freckled cheek. Does everyone live like this? I can't ask at school. If word spreads about what happens at home, it will make the beltings worse. But everything will get better. It has to. I just have to put my plan into action.

Tonight. Tonight I will do it.

I slip on my riding boots and head over to the stables. I give the four horses extra feed, fill their water tubs, rub each one on the nose and whisper, 'Goodbye.' On my way back to the house, I pluck a few oranges from the gnarly old fruit trees in the garden.

After a dinner of Spaghetti Bolognese, because that's what I'm best at, my father slumps on the lounge watching television, a collection of empty wine bottles and beer cans littering the carpet at his feet. The stench of cigarette smoke fills the room. Some people smoke outside. Not him. I take a few slices of bread and cheese from the kitchen, not too much —too obvious—especially since Dad rarely buys food and spends so much money at the pub.

I go to my room, feigning tiredness, and climb into bed fully dressed. Clothes that cover my limbs aren't a problem in winter but in summer, that's another story. At least the school in our small mountain village doesn't have a uniform, so when I was younger, everyone just thought I was a tomboy who liked wearing RM Williams work shirts and jeans. It's more difficult now that I travel into Littleton for high school. I remember the countless nights of falling asleep in fear. No more.

Finally, Dad stumbles along the hall to his bedroom.

I wait to hear him snore and soon the deep sounds become rhythmical. He won't wake until morning; he rarely does these days.

I rise, pick up my backpack stuffed with clothes and food, take the torch from the bedside and move noiselessly across the room. A thousand memories tumble in my mind as I grab a small photo of Mum from the dressing table and slip it into my bag.

'Sorry, Mum,' I whisper. 'He's worse since you died. But things will get better. I'll find your old school friend, Bernadette O'Hara. She'll look after me.'

I slide out the back door and stumble on the wooden steps. *Pick yourself up. Keep going.* I move out to the gravel road as quickly as I can while the full moon lights the way. *Don't use your torch unless you have to. Don't draw attention to yourself.*

A small herd of cattle move restlessly among a clump of trees. In the distance, a dingo howls. *Keep going. Don't stop now.*

I'm almost in the village. *Be careful. Tread quietly. Don't jump at shadows.*

Eventually the road will snake down the mountain through the remnants of ancient rainforest, across the valley floor to Hopeton, the Big River town far away. I yawn. I'd really like to stop at Mrs Johnson's house and sleep on the front veranda but it's too risky.

I've tried telling Mrs Johnson what's happening at home but the old woman only said, 'Now, dear, you mustn't tell stories. Your father is a good man.'

I wanted to scream at her, 'It isn't a story! Look! See my bruises! Why do you think I'm always wearing long sleeved tops and jeans?' But what was the point? Fifteen-year-old girls rarely argue with old ladies and Mum taught me better manners than that. Anyway, what could Mrs Johnson do? Her bird-like figure is no match for my father.

I pass the village school, its roof gleaming in the moonlight, the playground equipment unoccupied. So many happy times there, before my life changed, before Mum died, before Dad started blaming everything on me, their only child. No one at the high school will miss me. I'm often away these days. I told my roll teacher and friends that I'm going away for a week to visit a sick aunt. I don't have an aunt, let alone a sick one, but they don't know that. No one will check; it sounds believable enough.

Weak rays of sunlight peep over the horizon. *Keep going, don't let anyone see you.* Hunger gnaws at me. I pause by a road bridge and take an orange from my backpack, peel off the pebbly rind with my thumbs and fingers, devour the fruit. Juice dribbles down my chin.

I need to wash the stickiness from my fingers so I veer off to the left and pick my way through stunted bushes and head towards the reedy creek. Crouching down, I wash my hands and fill the water bottle.

Along the road, tall gums stand to attention. A magpie flaps across the landscape. Bracken fern wave in the morning air.

There's a rumble in the distance. It's getting louder, coming this way. What is it? Who is it? It's only about a kilometre away now so I scramble under the bridge and curl myself into a ball. The vehicle slows. The smell of cow manure and urine wafts through the air. A cattle truck. Has the driver seen me? *Don't move, wait.*

A belching noise, grinding of gears and the vehicle rattles across the narrow wooden planks overhead and travels on. I wait a few minutes until there's no engine noise and emerge from my hiding place.

It's still early, Dad won't be up yet, not after the amount of alcohol he drank last night. If I'm lucky, he won't wake until about the time the school bus comes and he'll assume that I've already left for school.

Find the abandoned rail line, follow it down the mountain. Get away. Keep going.

Pink lantana flowers sprinkle the hillside as I make my way across to the old derelict railway station a couple of kilometres past the village. Trains stopped using the line over twenty years ago; now whisky grass grows between the abandoned tracks. Cream paint peels from the station building, dust and vermin inhabiting it.

Water tanks stand high on pedestals beside the line, unused since the time of steam trains. Black scribblings randomly adorn one wall. Someone called Dylan signed his name on a guard rail, vandalizing it. Some boys have no brains.

Keep going, follow the silver line to a better life.

I'm out in the open now. Will someone see me? I move fast; soon the school bus will go by. *Reach the trees, find where the railway enters the bush.* A stony track runs parallel. Use that. It's easier to follow than walking between the lines, stepping on or between old sleepers, their wood rotting.

I push on. Magpies scold me from the branches above. Are the birds planning to attack? Lifting my backpack onto my head, I hurry on to safety.

An hour or so later, I stop by the side of the track, gulp a few mouthfuls from my water bottle and remove the squashed cheese sandwiches from my bag. They're thin and misshapen but nourishment nonetheless. My body aches from tiredness. I move away from the track over to a clearing in the bush and slump against the trunk of a blackbutt tree. *Just sit here for a while, get your strength back …*

When I wake, the sun is high. I swallow the last of my water, peel another orange and bury the rind. *Hide the evidence. Stick to the plan.* I head over to the track and trek on.

Time passes and finally, Wild Cattle Creek is ahead. I thread my way down to the water's edge, pushing aside low stunted bushes and bracken fern that whip back onto my legs.

Something on the path ahead catches my eye. I stop abruptly, frozen, transfixed, heart pounding, adrenaline pumping.

Silence. A red-bellied black snake is sunning itself on the track ahead. It lies there, motionless. Fear knifes me. What should I do? Should I wait? How long? Should I turn and run? Throw a stick in its direction? Mum told me that if you don't threaten snakes, they won't hurt you. But what if this one does? I don't want to die alone in the bush.

Maintaining my gaze on the snake, I step backwards. My foot crunches on a stick, the sound echoing in the silence.

The serpent lifts its head and turns towards me. I scream and leap backwards. The snake slithers away.

I retrace my steps up the embankment. Now what?

My heart's still thumping but I need water. I wait ten minutes and then, breathing heavily, gingerly tread the path down to the water's edge where I hesitate. Who or what made the rough track? Cattle? Kangaroos? People? Scanning my surroundings, my senses are on alert. A lizard suns itself on a log and plops into the creek. I hastily fill my water bottle, gulp half and fill it again.

All afternoon, I trudge on. *Keep going. Don't stop.*

Thunderheads hang in the sky, gathering, menacing, heavy with rain. Soon, there's a loud rumbling noise, like a giant dancing on the iron roof at home. Lightning forks across the sky.

I run and stumble my way to a railway bridge and hide underneath. Wind batters the landscape and throws rain like gravel, pelting the ground. Dark squalls rip in and the wind screams. I huddle underneath the bridge.

Don't be afraid. Don't panic. It won't last. Cover your eyes so you don't see the lightning. Or cover your ears so you don't hear the thunder? Which?

By the time the storm passes, it's almost dark. *Stay here undercover, safe and dry.* I flatten the grass and ferns around me, eat the last of my fruit, plump up the backpack for a pillow and before long, sleep envelop s me.

I wake with a start. What time is it? My father would have started searching but I'm long gone. Hopefully, he thought I was at school yesterday and didn't realize I was missing until the afternoon bus passed the farm gate.

He's not going to call me 'useless' or 'gutless' again and he'll find out soon enough that he'll be cooking his own dinner. No more being belted or slammed against a wall or having a chair thrown at my head. All because I might have burnt the vegetables for dinner or dropped a heavy feed bucket or been too slow to open a gate or fallen off one of the horses when it was spooked.

I pick up my backpack and set off. It's still early and I'm hungry.

A few kilometres on stands a brick chimney, the remains of an old farm cottage. Some fruit trees still grow in the tangled thicket of a garden, lemons and oranges. A passionfruit vine attaches itself to a tall bush. Food! I snatch oranges from the lower branches, eat three and stow the others in my bag. In the distance, a car travels south towards Littleton. Not me.

I continue east. *Stay close to the edge of the bush. Avoid the main road. Don't draw attention to yourself. Keep going.*

All day I duck and weave until I move through the safety of the afternoon shadows. Houses wink with yellow lights as evening closes in.

On the edge of Hopeton, I search for a sign to point me the right way. Not sure where Bernadette lives, my best option is to wait for her at the stables where she keeps her horses. I approach the racecourse, climb through the closed metal gate and follow the road around to the far side. A few thoroughbreds whinny as I pass along the row of stables. The horses are fed, watered, rugged. There's no one else here. I find an empty stable and settle myself down for another night.

I wake to the soft neighs of the horses. Someone's coming. Who? I scramble to my feet and move to the stable door. Bernadette! She approaches with a thin boy, a stable hand or jockey.

I step out of the shadows. She looks at me in shock. 'Kate! What are you doing here?'

I tell her everything, about Dad, how he changed after Mum

died, how my life has been.

Bernadette puts her arm around me. 'You poor girl,' she soothes. As she holds me close, I bump into her bulging stomach, hidden under a loose top.

'You're pregnant!' I exclaim.

Her face lights up. 'Yes, finally. IVF.' She pats her stomach. 'I need to be careful so no more riding for a while. In fact, I'm selling the horses.'

My shoulders slump. 'Oh. I thought maybe I could work for you here. And live with you.'

'I'm sorry, Kate. I'm giving up training. And we only live in a small flat. Once the baby comes, there won't be room for anyone else.'

What now? Where do I go now?

Bernadette's eyes roam my face. 'Are you sure you want to work with horses?'

I nod. 'Yes, I'm sure.'

'Well, I might be able to arrange something. Kate, you wait here while I make a few phone calls.'

Ten minutes later, Bernadette returns. 'I think I've found the perfect place.' She smiles and continues, 'There's a trainer down the coast, Mary Jackson. She's getting too old to ride herself and she needs company in the house. Mary says you can stay with her in return for some help around the stables. What do you think?'

I don't know this trainer, this Mary Jackson. But I do know Bernadette. If Mum's best friend, my old babysitter and neighbour, thinks it's the perfect place, maybe it is. Maybe it isn't.

Take a chance. 'Yes, thank you.' Anything would be better than living with my father.

I catch a train south, towards Mary Jackson, and imagine a better future.

Wallpaper

R. A. Stephens

The party will be on Friday night. I know everyone is going because I saw the flyer being passed around. No one passed it to me. Why would they? I just hang out in the corner that I've made my space since I arrived in town. It's a country town and I don't know anyone, but that's my fault—not theirs.

I sit by myself at the school lunch tables and wonder if I should try talking to someone. I have been at the school for about two months and everyone was friendly to start with, but I could really only manage the occasional 'hi'. People slowly started to walk away and go back to their groups. They weren't mean; I just didn't communicate, didn't know what to say.

'Where did you live before?'

'The city.'

'Oh yeah, what brought you out here?'

'Mum's job.'

'Do you play sport?'

'No.'

'Do you like music?'

'Sometimes.'

'What sort?'

'You know …'

'What do you like doing?'

'You know … normal stuff.'

The questions always came. My short, blunt answers were all I could manage. They would probe for more information, like: 'What are the schools like in the city?'

'Big,' is all I would say.

No matter how much I tried, I couldn't seem to get out more words than enough to satisfy that I didn't ignore them. Sometimes people would sit with me. They were nice, don't get me wrong, but then they would just talk to each other as I offered nothing.

One day I bought a packet of chips to share—Mum told me it would help. Everyone chatted nicely around the table as normal. I couldn't complain. There was even a sea of thank yous at the end and I forced a smile. *See? That was easy.* At home that night, I didn't tell Mum that I still didn't talk. She just assumed I did and chatted happily about how it was a good thing, and wasn't I glad she suggested it? After all, I never got a word in edgewise, even if I had something to say.

I gravitated to the table furthest from the action about three weeks in. And that's where I stayed. Sometimes I brought a book, sometimes I just sat, sometimes I would dream about flying away. We weren't allowed our phones, not that I would have done anything except listen to music if I had mine. Sometimes I fed the pigeons, even though I knew I probably shouldn't. They would show off their tails to one another; even for them it seemed easy to communicate.

At least I was fitting in in class. Maths is fun; so is science most of the time—but we have to work in groups a little too often and that gets awkward. I just do as I am told and don't bother asking for help. I need to learn maths and science to train in aviation.

And I got a job. I found one washing dishes at the local hotel.

Pretty easy. They just pile the dishes and I put them in the dishwasher, and they get put back out. They love me there because they know I won't get distracted talking to everyone. It's boring, but worth it for flying lessons.

I can hear the ringing of Mum's voice. 'Just speak up and ask them!' Oh so obvious, right? She's never felt the sting of sitting in a room full of people with no one knowing you were there. She's always loud and right there so anyone could see and hear her. I just sat in the corner. Like always. Disappearing into the wallpaper. Sometimes that is exactly what I felt like. Wallpaper.

But for the first time in two months, I wanted to do something that everyone else was doing. I wanted to be a part of the group. I wanted to go to the party—it had nothing to do with books, flying or music, but my social craving surfaced. *Why now?* I couldn't answer. Five people in our class had just got their license and apparently this was a reason to celebrate. Everyone talked about the last one. A party is something most teens wouldn't think twice about going to. Me, however …

The girls hosting it, Charlie, Olivia and Hayley, had been the first to speak to me. They were nice, so I was pretty sure they wouldn't mind, but I had no idea how to ask them.

The day before the party I notice an invite in my locker. Feels odd. Charlie sees me holding it and smiles.

'Come,' she mouths.

How can she still want me to come? I haven't spoken to her in six weeks, not after the first couple of weeks when questions were being fired at me.

Just speak up and talk to her.

She walks by and says, 'Seriously, come! Everyone is.'

'Ummm, sure,' is all I can manage.

The problem with being intolerably socially awkward: I crave human attention, but I have no idea what to say. If I say the wrong thing, will someone think I am a weirdo? Will they think I am a weirdo if I don't say anything anyway? What if I talk too fast or too slow? If I actually start talking, will I ever be able to stop—just like Mum?

So, I just let them call me shy.

I am not sure if it is that. Seems that way, but it isn't that I am afraid of them; I just don't know what to say. I forget to even open my mouth. What could I say that adds to the conversation, that doesn't just repeat what has already been said? Maybe when I finally say something, it will mean something. So why not go to the party? It won't be much different from school; I can just disappear like wallpaper. I am good at it. At least it beats being wallpaper at home.

I get dressed and show Mum the invite. I don't even say anything, she just gets excited and starts fluttering around while chatting to herself. I still don't know how she doesn't notice that I hardly ever speak when it is just her and me. She's a good mum, just the opposite of me. She isn't afraid of anything.

'Now make sure you stay out of trouble at the party, not that I think you would do anything crazy. There won't be any alcohol, right? Of course not, the kids around here are really good and I know Charlie's mum and she will keep the party safe. But if anyone sneaks it in, you know to say no, don't you, darling?' She looks at me for a second and I just nod as I know I won't have time to get a word in before she continues.

'Okay, so you should wear that new dress we got the other day, it looks so good on you. Very appropriate. I am so glad you are talking to new friends now. I was really worried when we first came that it would be hard for you to make friends given how quiet you are—which I never understood. I mean, quiet in my family—who knew.'

She pauses and I wonder what more she has to say as I can see she is thinking—which so rarely happens in the middle of an exposé.

132

'You know, I was shy once too. Actually no, I wasn't shy. I just didn't know what to say. I was younger than you, though, when I did start talking and then I just didn't stop … as you know.' She laughs at herself, not waiting for me to laugh or smile. 'Maybe you are just a late bloomer. But yay! Have fun, darling.'

She keeps chattering away as she helps me dress. I want to tell her I am sixteen and can dress myself, but hey, whatever. I never mind Mum's chattering, it fills the quiet and makes it easier for me to not have to talk. It gives me comfort that she wasn't always a natural at talking. Maybe I should try, just a little.

6pm. Time for the party.

There are a few pigeons showing off as we walk outside and climb in the car. Mum fits the L plate on so I can drive. I think about how much more fun it will be to learn to fly than to drive. Not long now. Flying doesn't involve talking to too many people—at least not that often, just when you tell them when the plane is landing and so on.

I add a whole ten minutes to my logbook.

'Call me when you want to get picked up,' Mum yells from the car. 'Any time is fine!'

I smile and wave. She is good to me. Now, can I learn to say more than normal? Maybe? Well, I am here.

I practice using my voice. It feels dry. I don't think I've spoken all afternoon. *Had Mum noticed?*

Charlie comes to greet me. Before she speaks I manage to say: 'Thank you for inviting me.'

'Oh, I am so glad you came, Abs—can I call you that? It's easier to say than Abigail.'

'Um, sure.'

'Call me Charlz, now that you've been to my house. Charlotte is way too formal and Charlie is starting to sound like I am still five. I have my license now! When do you get yours?'

Time to speak. Give more than a date. Say something.

'Well, I turn seventeen in a few months, but I want to get my pilot license more.'

'Oh wow, really? Haylz has hers! You should talk to her about it. She did her lessons down on Aerodrome Road.'

'That's where I want to go. I have my first lesson booked in next week.'

'Oh, that's exciting.'

Charlz stops talking for a bit while she grabs a drink. Mum will be pleased … it's just lemonade. She offers one to me and I say thanks. I have now said over twenty-five words. Let's see if I can get it to one hundred tonight.

Someone once told me that girls speak thousands of words a day. I might write that many, but I definitely don't say them. Mum speaks ten times more than anyone, so I always figured she made up for it. But let's see.

'Hey, Haylz and Livs.' Everyone apparently ends with a 's' or 'z' sound around here.

'Abs wants to be a pilot too!'

'Oh, that's cool.'

'It's so good you came!'

'You can host the party when you get your pilot license!'

They all start talking at once and though I can keep up, I can't say much. I start to shrink back. I can see the corner. The flowery dress Mum picked out for me will be a great addition to the wallpaper.

'So, Abs.' Haylz pauses, 'Hey you're one of us now!' She grabs me and pulls me away from the wall. No wallpaper for me this time.

'Tell us why you want to fly. I wanted to fly because I want to have more independence and one of my pilot friends said he wants to fly because he wants to fly commercial planes one day. I don't want to do that, I'm just doing it for fun. What about you?'

'Well, I like the freedom. I also like the wind and the way

things float on it. I want to fly one of those small planes and have lots of control.' They look at me, willing me to go on. It gives my confidence a little boost and I keep going. 'Like, when I normally stay out of the way. I know I'm a bit weird, but I imagine myself as wallpaper and stay out of the way. I think being a part of the clouds, trees and birds would be a bit like that. A part of the ceiling.'

'Oh, that's amazing. Are you a writer too?' Livs looks at me, waiting for a reply.

'I do like to write—you know, at my corner table.'

'Well, I am so glad you came to tell us. I want someone else to go flying with one day, and I'm so sick of all the boys. We can go together once you have your license!'

Haylz looks genuine. More than I thought. These girls are for real.

I don't talk much but just listen to them throughout the night. I meet some of the others, including the "popular group", who are a bit more pretentious but aren't too bad as long as I say more than one-word answers. I'm pretty sure they think I am a weirdo, but suddenly that doesn't matter anymore.

I call Mum to pick me up around eleven.

'Thanks for coming, Abs. Sit with us at lunch on Monday.'

'I will.' It's a short reply, but I mean it.

'Yeah, you're cool.'

'Yeah, we just thought you didn't like us.'

It was never about them. Always about me. But I think it might be better to be weird and speak than to be weird and wallpaper. And just maybe … maybe I did have something to say.

Izzy's Swing

Kate Gordon

It had been such a long time since she saw these trees.

She remembered, now, the look of the light—like mercury dripping through the leaves. And that magpie—she was sure that was the same one. It had that same look about it. She still had the scar on her shoulder from where its beak had connected.

'Are you watching me, magpie?' she whispered. 'Did you think the same thing? That you'd never see me again?'

'Who are you talking to?' asked Izzy.

Eva's breath snagged in her throat. She had almost forgotten her small sister was there. She had tried to forget, despite the hot little hand clutched tightly in hers.

She had tried to forget what she was here to do.

Again, she cursed her mother. What sort of parent foists a job like this on a fifteen-year-old girl? What sort of mother wouldn't want to be here, to do it herself?

Especially now. Especially after everything.

'Nobody, Izz,' Eva said.

'Were you talking to the bird?' asked Izzy.

Eva looked up at the tree again. The magpie was looking down at her, its fire-orange eyes seeking hers. Eva squeezed Izzy's hand. 'Yeah, maybe,' she said. She peered down at her sister, so small, round-cheeked, with hair like a sunrise. 'Does that make me mad, do you think?'

Izzy shook her head. 'No.'

Eva tried to keep walking, but Izzy stopped her, tugging on her hand.

Ahead, through the line of eucalypts that guarded the fence, the school building crouched in wait—tall and dark and menacing. At least, Eva assumed that's how it must seem to Izzy.

It was how it seemed, just a little bit, to her, too.

The smell of the eucalypts drifted over on the breeze like a warning.

Eva's body slackened. 'What is it, Izz?' she asked. But she knew, of course. She knew this would happen. She had told their mother this would happen.

'I don't want to,' Izzy said, softly.

Eva tried pulling her hand but of course that wouldn't work. Izzy was a statue. Maybe she could have tried harder—their mother would have said to just pick her up and go. 'She's five years old,' she would have snapped. 'Just make her do it.'

But that was the thing, wasn't it?

Izzy was only five years old.

Eva remembered Izzy's first day of kinder, only a year before, how she'd hidden behind Eva's legs. 'No, no, no, Eva,' she had whispered, over and over. 'No, no, no, I don't want to. I don't want to go in there. It's not safe in there.'

And Eva had been able, then, that time, to crouch to Izzy's height and ruffle those sunrise curls and say, 'Izzy, I promise you. I promise you, it's safe in there. It's a school. It's the safest place you can be.'

And Izzy had been able to run her own small hands through

Eva's hair—sun-kissed brown and straight as button grass; had been able to kiss Eva on her wide, freckled nose; had been able to breathe in her sister and fill her lungs with calm and safety.

And her teacher, Mrs Fox, had been able to scoop Izzy into her warm, soft arms, and say the same thing: 'Izzy, I promise you, it's safe.'

Izzy had been happy with that—with those two, truthful promises. With the two promises that could be kept.

But now …

The magpie above them in the ghost gum tree squawked, and it felt like a warning. Felt like an admonishment. Felt like a judgement. Because Izzy was a stone and she was a statue and she would not go and, no matter what their mother said, Eva could not make her.

Because she could not promise, this time.

So, instead, Eva sighed and she squeezed Izzy's hand and she said, 'Come on,' and when Izzy opened her mouth to protest, Eva said, 'No, not come on there—come this way, with me.'

And she took Izzy away, across the road, to the small, deserted playground. To Izzy's favourite swing set.

'What's happening, Evie? What's happening?' Izzy said.

'You're swinging,' Eva said, with a sigh, 'and I will tell you a story.'

Izzy looked puzzled. 'But Mummy —"

'Is not here,' said Eva, through gritted teeth. 'So, we are going to the playground and you are swinging, and I will tell you a story.'

'With once upon a time?'

Eva nodded. 'Yes.'

And Izzy seemed happy with that.

In the park, they were alone, and it was quiet. Only the swing squeaked a little, but that felt like a comfort—Izzy's favourite swing always squeaked just like that.

Above them, a magpie landed on a tree branch. 'That's the same one,' Izzy said, looking up. 'He's following us.'

'Yeah,' said Eva. 'Maybe.'

Izzy looked back down to meet her eye. 'Push?' she asked.

Eva stood behind her, pulled on the metal chains of the swing, and let go. Izzy let out a gleeful whoop. It made Eva's heart hurt. She sounded so small, and so free.

'Once upon a time?' Izzy prodded, her tiny legs pumping, pumping—it was a new skill and she was so proud of it.

Eva looked up at the tree, met the magpie's amber eyes, heard the wind in the leaves around it. 'Did you know,' she said to Izzy, 'that what we call magpies in Australia aren't really magpies at all?'

'That's not once upon a time,' Izzy protested.

Eva sighed. 'Once upon a time,' she said, 'there was a young magpie …'

'What was his name?'

'Her name,' Eva corrected, 'was Isobel.'

'That's my name!' Izzy said, happily, slapping her knees.

'It is.'

'Birds can be called Isobel, too?'

'They can. Anyhow, this magpie was not like her brothers and sisters. They loved to fly, leaping out of the nest every morning to follow their mother into the sky, to join the other magpies, circling and stealing leaves and playing with sticks and rocks. But Isobel was frightened. She knew that there were raptors who flew in the sky with the magpies—'

'Raptors? Like dinosaurs?'

Eva laughed. Izzy loved dinosaurs. They never scared her. She was fearless when it came to dinosaurs and all other monsters, too. Usually, monsters didn't scare Izzy. Lately, mostly everything did. Not dinosaurs, though, still.

'Not velociraptors,' Eva corrected. 'Raptors are birds of prey. Hunter birds. Like eagles and hawks.'

Izzy paused in her swinging. She shuddered. 'Scary,' she whispered.

Eva gave her a little push. The chain rattled and squeaked. 'Yeah. Isobel in the story thought the same. And for good reason. She knew that the raptors hunted magpies. Sometimes they caught them. Sometimes they killed them. One of her siblings had been killed by a raptor, a long time ago.'

'No!'

Eva nodded. *'So, Isobel—because of her fear—stayed in the nest every day, watching her siblings fly around and play and have fun. She wished she could join them, but she couldn't risk it. She couldn't risk being killed by the raptor.*

One day, her mother had had enough. She landed in the nest and she said, 'Isobel, you have to leave here. You have to join us, up in the sky.' 'But it's not safe in the sky,' Isobel told her. It's only safe here.' Her mother put a wing around her baby girl and said, 'Life is not safe. If you stay in the nest forever, you're not living. Life is about taking risks. Life is about flying.' Isobel thought for a long while, after her mother said that. She looked down at her brothers and sisters, who were playing with a gum nut. It did look fun.

Finally, she said, 'Will you protect me, up in the sky?' Her mother ruffled her daughter's downy feathers. 'Always,' she said. 'Until you are big enough to have your own babies and protect them. I will always be in the sky beside you, between you and the danger.'

And so, finally, Isobel bravely left the nest. She flew under her mother's wing, and her mother protected her, always. And in the sky, Isobel finally felt herself. She finally felt free. And her brothers and sisters and friends were so happy to see her and play with her again. Soon, Isobel forgot to be afraid. Except for when the shadow of the raptors could be seen, overhead. Then she ran back to her mother and her mother protected her, every time."

Eva finally took a breath. Izzy had stopped swinging to listen. 'The end?' she whispered.

Eva nodded. 'The end.'

'But ... then what?' Izzy said, standing up. 'Was Isobel safe always? What about when her mother died? And what if ... what if there was a magpie whose mother didn't protect them? And what if there were too many raptors and you never knew when the raptors would come? What if there was a grandmother magpie who got eaten by a raptor instead? What if ...?' Izzy's eyes were wet now, and then her cheeks.

Eva sighed. She meant for the story to have a different meaning for her tiny sister. She meant for it to help her sister be brave. Instead, it seemed to have done the opposite thing.

'Maybe ...' she said, slowly, weakly, 'if Isobel didn't have a mother to protect her, she had a sister. 'And maybe the grandmother ... maybe the grandmother ...'

Eva couldn't stop her own tears from coming, as she thought of her grandmother's soap-and-ginger smell. As she thought of the shadowy threat that had taken her. The real hunter. The real monster. The sickness that had stolen the breath from her lungs. She thought of how their school had closed, to protect them from the sickness. She thought of how she had felt safe, for a little while.

Now, she did not feel safe. Now, she felt as though there were monsters in every dark corner. She couldn't protect Izzy like the mother magpie if she always felt this scared.

And her mother, when their grandmother died, had turned into a stone statue, just like Izzy on the way to school. So, it was up to Eva. And Eva ... Eva was fifteen. She did not know what to do.

'Are you scared, too?' Izzy whispered.

Eva knew she should say, 'No!' and smile and pretend everything was fine. But everything was not fine and they both knew it and she didn't know how to lie.

She nodded. 'I'm scared, Izzy.'

'But we have to go because that's living?' Izzy said, quietly.

'And ... our friends are there,' Eva added. 'Amelia is there. She's missed you.'

'We play with rocks, sometimes,' Izzy said. 'Sometimes leaves, too.'

They both looked up at the magpie in the tree. It was still watching them. Eva remembered how the magpie—maybe that magpie—had swooped at her. How it had made the cut and the cut was now a scar. It didn't hurt any more but the memory of it did, and yet …

She wasn't afraid of this magpie. This magpie … it felt as if it was protecting her. The magpie who swooped must have been a child if it was the same. This one …

Suddenly, she had an idea. She pointed at the magpie. 'That one,' she told her sister. 'That's Isobel.'

Izzy squinted up at the tree. 'Grown-up Isobel?'

Eva nodded. 'And she has no babies, so she's protecting us, instead.'

'From … everything?' Izzy asked.

Eva nodded.

Izzy thought for a moment. Then, she said, 'Okay.'

Eva sat down on the swing beside Izzy. She breathed in the smell of the park—cut grass and barbecue and sunscreen and daisies. They sat like that, two sisters, side-by-side, for a long time. The park was quiet. The park felt safe. Outside of its walls, everything was chaos and fear and more risk than the open sky. Eva wanted to stay in the park forever.

'I wonder if I can swing by myself,' Izzy said, finally.

'Probably,' Eva replied. 'You are a big five-year-old now.'

'Mummy always says I should try and do it myself. She says I should try and do lots of things by myself. Because I'm big now.'

'She does say that.'

'I like you pushing me, though,' Izzy said.

'I like pushing you,' said Eva.

'Maybe even when I'm really big, you'll do it.' It was a question, even though it didn't sound like one.

'Always,' said Eva. 'I'll always push you.'

'Now?' asked Izzy, hopefully.

Distantly, Eva could hear the school bell ringing. They should both be in class now. Soon, their teachers would notice their absence and call their mother and she would be angry.

But this time, beneath the gum tree, beneath the magpie, feeling so sacred, somehow. Just a small, perfect pocket of safety. And love. Eva wasn't ready to let it go, just yet.

'Now,' she told Izzy.

She stood and moved behind her. She looked up at the magpie one more time. And it seemed like the magpie nodded, and it wasn't the case of course—the magpie was only a magpie—but it felt like permission.

Eva pulled on the metal chains.

And she let go.

And Izzy flew.

Author Bios

D.J. Blackmore

'There's nothing more peaceful than the sound of sixty-thousand bees busily making honey.' D. J. Blackmore is a beekeeper, simple-living advocate and mother of five, yet stories are her oldest love. Life experiences are a wonderful inspiration for writing books, characters met or tales shared. While artists are often seen as oblivious to the outside world, she believes it is only because they see what the rest of the world fails to notice. She pens contemporary and historical adult and young adult fiction, her debut novel, *Charter to Redemption* translated into the language of the Czech Republic.

Sandy Bigna

Sandy Bigna loves reading, writing and talking (to anyone who will listen!) about children's literature, with her passion being young adult literature. Studying children's literature at the University of Canberra and working as a children's librarian inspired her love of children's and YA literature. The highlight of her writing life was having her YA manuscript *Exposed* shortlisted for the Matilda Children's Literature Prize in 2020 (Harper Collins Australia). Along with her love of writing and reading, Sandy also enjoys reviewing kids book on her Instagram page (you can find her at @aussie_kids_books) and being a soccer mum to her three young boys!

Geraldine Borella

Geraldine Borella writes stories for children and adults and has been published in magazines, online, in podcasts and anthologies. Her stories feature in *Spooktacular Stories – Thrilling Tales for Brave Kids*; *Short and Twisted*, 2016; literary magazine page seventeen, issue 11; and on Antipodean SF's website and podcast. In 2018, she won an ASA Emerging Writer's mentorship and placed second in the Buzz Words Short Story Prize for Children. She came second in the 2020 Just Write For Kids Pitch It! Competition pitching the young adult novel she is currently working on. She lives on the Atherton Tablelands in Far North Queensland.

Samantha-Ellen Bound

Sam-Ellen Bound is a writer, editor and children's author. From humble beginnings as an eight-year old writing *Goosebumps* rip-offs, she now has many years experience working with books—as an author, bookseller, reviewer, editor, production and marketing coordinator, in education, you name it!

Sam-Ellen has been shortlisted for numerous short story awards, including most recently the Peter Carey Short Story Award. She was shortlisted for the Vogel Prize in 2018. Her first novel *What the Raven Saw* was published in 2013. The first book in her four-part middle-grade fantasy series, *Seven Wherewithal Way*, will be published in 2021.

Niko Campbell-Ellis

Niko Campbell-Ellis was born and raised in Tasmania, amongst farms which inspired the setting for her story in this collection. She now lives on the New South Wales mid north coast where she works as a teacher. Niko loves ocean swimming, cooking, reading, and, of course, writing. She has a Master of Children's Literature from Macquarie University and is passionate about the role of literature in young people's lives. Niko writes for children and adults and has had short stories published in *The School Magazine*, the *Hunter Writer's Centre's Grieve Anthology*, the *Newcastle Herald*, *Seizure Online Magazine*, and *The Quarry Journal*.

Peter Clarkson

Peter Clarkson is a philosophy teacher who lives in Melbourne with his beautiful wife and three amazing daughters. When he's not running marathons or philosophising, he likes to write stories for children. His stories raise questions about our experience of reality, what we can know and take for granted. He is a huge fan of Roald Dahl and C. S. Lewis and any tale where the familiar and ordinary is made strange and wonderful.

Kelly Emmerton

Kelly Emmerton has written fiction for as long as she can remember. She considers storytelling one of the most important ways of connecting with people and has channeled that passion into a professional career as a copywriter. In her fiction work, she writes across genres including realism, sci-fi and fantasy and has been published in and edited multiple short story fiction anthologies. Kelly studied a Bachelor of Comms. with Honours, majoring in Writing and Cultural studies at the University of Technology, Sydney.

Carla Fitzgerald

Carla Fitzgerald is a writer, a recovered lawyer and a mum of three, from Sydney.

Her debut middle-grade novel is due for release in June 2022 and she also has a picture book coming out, titled, *Keeping Up with the Dachshunds*.

Carla is a proud *Books in Homes* Role Model and a Coach with the Harding Miller Education Foundation.

Kate Gordon

Kate Gordon grew up in a small town by the sea in Tasmania. She is the author of six novels for teenagers, as well as the picture books, *Bird on a Wire* and *Amira's Magpie*, and the junior fiction series, *Juno Jones*. She now writes middle grade fiction. *The Heartsong of Wonder Quinn* was a notable book in the 2020 CBCA Awards. *Aster's Good, Right Things* was shortlisted in the CBCA Awards. Kate was shortlisted in the Dorothy Hewett Awards for an Unpublished Manuscript, and was commended in the 2018 Vogel's Awards. Her books have been published internationally and adapted for the stage. When not writing, Kate reads, listens to Josh Ritter, has grand adventures with her daughter and is learning to ride a bike.

Deborah Huff-Horwood

Deborah Huff-Horwood is an emerging writer from Canberra, vigorously pursuing her new career. She works from her lakefront eyrie to create imaginative and evocative children's picture books, middle-grade fiction, short stories and poems. Her stories centre upon themes of courage and resilience. Deborah has a wealth of life experience after having been a primary school teacher for seventeen years, a certified pastry chef working in fine dining, a BA-trained visual artist, and a theatrical costume designer. Her full-time commitment to writing, both for children and for adults, is reflected in the seventeen awards, short- and long-listings that she has received in thirteen months, including Highly Commended for the AAWP-Ubud Writers and Readers Festival 2020, Emerging Writers' Prize. She is being published in seven Australian anthologies. Deborah has two adult children, is an avid op-shopper and adores rocky, windswept beaches.

Elizabeth Macintosh

Elizabeth Macintosh is a former teacher based in regional NSW. Although she has published articles in newspapers and national magazines, her main interests are writing for children and YA. Elizabeth's tales often contain an element of danger and many are inspired by real places or events. Her short stories have been published in *The School Magazine* and several anthologies, including *The Creative Kids Tales Story Collection 2* and the *Tell 'em They're Dreaming Anthology*.

Elizabeth presents writing workshops and author talks in schools and public libraries, as well as speaking at community dinners connected with writers' festivals.

Laura Norris

Laura Norris studied Creative Writing and Literature at Griffith University, where her short story, *Dancing with Knives*, was published in the annual student anthology, *Talent Implied 2019*. She is a co-owner of The Mad Hatters Bookshop, an independent bookstore in Manly, Queensland, where she can be found championing the incredible Brisbane writing community and throwing books at people.

Frances Prentice

Writing her first poem at age eight, Frances has been an avid reader and writer for her whole life. Some unexpected time out of the rat race during COVID in 2020, and the prompting of a supportive friend, encouraged her to follow her dream to be a published author. In 2020, Frances was successful in writing a bush ballad to be included in the *Tell 'em They're Dreaming Anthology* published by *Share Your Story* and was one of four finalists whose short stories were published in the *Audrey Magazine* (Issue 18). She is currently working on a novel for middle-grade students, and is honoured to be included in this publication.

R. A. Stephens

R. A. is a teacher by day, writer, editor and publisher by night. She is passionate about the written word, what stories can do to take a reader to a new world and open our eyes to love, compassion, the bigger picture and much more. When not working, teaching or writing, she enjoys living in the country and spending time with her kids and cats.

Future Short Story Collections

This is the second Rhiza Edge themed short story collection for teens. If you are a writer and would like to contribute, please check out our submissions and themed calls for collections on our website: www.wombatrhiza.com.au.

Other titles:

Crossed Spaces (2021)
Lynne Stringer and R. A. Stephens (Editors)

Dust Makers (2022)
Penny Jaye and R. A. Stephens (Editors)

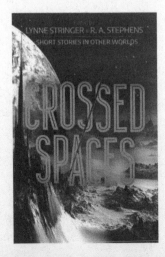
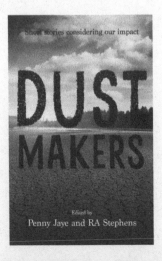